W9-BQZ-911

Emil and Karl

Yankev Glatshteyn

➤➤ • ⤛

Translated by
Jeffrey Shandler

A NEAL PORTER BOOK
ROARING BROOK PRESS
NEW MILFORD, CONNECTICUT

The original Yiddish edition of *Emil un Karl* was published in 1940
by Farlag M. S. Sklarsky, New York City. Permission to publish this
translation has kindly been granted by the estate of Fanny Mazel Glatstein.

Completion of this translation was made possible
thanks to a grant from the New York State Council on the Arts.

English translation copyright 2006 © by Jeffrey Shandler

A Neal Porter Book
Published by Roaring Brook Press
Roaring Brook Press is a division of Holtzbrinck Publishing Holdings Limited Partnership
143 West Street, New Milford, Connecticut 06776

All rights reserved

Distributed in Canada by H. B. Fenn and Company, Ltd.
Library of Congress Cataloging-in-Publication Data
Glatstein, Jacob, 1896-1971.
[Emil un Karl. English]
Emil and Karl / by Yankev Glatshteyn ; translated by Jeffrey Shandler.— 1st American ed.
p. cm.   "A Neal Porter Book."
Summary: In Vienna, Austria, in 1940, two nine-year-old boys, one Jewish and one
Aryan, are classmates and best friends when events of the Nazi occupation draw them
even closer together as they fight to survive and escape together.
ISBN-13: 978-1-59643-119-5   ISBN-10: 1-59643-119-9
1. World War, 1939-1945—Austria—Juvenile fiction. [1. World War, 1939-1945—
Austria—Fiction. 2. Best friends—Fiction. 3. Jews—Austria—Fiction. 4. Righteous
Gentiles in the Holocaust—Fiction. 5. Nazis—Fiction. 6. Vienna (Austria)—
History—20th century—Fiction. 7. Austria—History—1938-1945—Fiction.] I.
Shandler, Jeffrey, ill. II. Title.
PZ7.G4814372Emi 2006 [Fic]—dc22 2005026800

Roaring Brook Press books are available for special promotions and premiums.
For details, contact: Director of Special Markets, Holtzbrinck Publishers.

Book design by Jennifer Browne
Printed in the United States of America
First edition April 2006
2   4   6   8   10   9   7   5   3   1

Dedicated to my children:

Saul
Naomi
Gabriel

Y.G.

To the Reader

Imagine that it is 1940. You are a Jewish boy or girl living in New York, Chicago, Los Angeles, or some other large American city. Your parents, or perhaps your grandparents, weren't born in the United States, but are immigrants from Eastern Europe. They came to America from such countries as Russia, Poland, Romania, Lithuania, Latvia, or Hungary. Your parents and grandparents didn't grow up speaking English. Instead, their native tongue was Yiddish, a Jewish language then used by millions of Jews across Europe. There, your family spoke Yiddish at home and with other Jews in the towns where they grew up. They might also have gone to schools where they were taught the same subjects you study in school—history, mathematics, literature—in Yiddish.

Here in the United States, you go to a public school where you speak English during the day. But on afternoons and weekends you go to another school, where you learn to speak Yiddish. At this school you learn to sing folksongs in Yiddish and read stories in Yiddish about Jewish history and customs. At home you sometimes speak Yiddish with your parents, grandparents, and other relatives, and you might look at Yiddish newspapers or listen to Yiddish broadcasts on the radio with them.

These days your family is very troubled by news about what has been happening in Europe, especially to their families and friends living there. For years, Jews living in Germany have suffered from the persecutions of the Nazi regime, led by a dictator named Adolf Hitler. More recently, Nazi Germany occupied other countries—Austria and part of Czechoslovakia—where they have also made life especially hard for Jews. Then, in September 1939, Nazi Germany invaded Poland, and a terrible war broke out across Europe. The situation is very grim for Jews and other people persecuted by the Nazis; their future is unclear.

One day, your teacher at the Yiddish school presents you and your classmates with a new book. It is different from the other Yiddish books you have been reading there. The new book tells a story about events that took place very recently, just months before the war in Europe began. The story isn't about dictators or armies. It's about two boys who are about the same age as you. The book describes what it is like to live in a place that is about to go to war, a place where ordinary people's lives are already being disrupted. Families are broken up, and many of them are losing their homes. People are being beaten and arrested. They aren't free to live as they wish or even to speak their minds, especially if they disagree with the government. Sometimes it is dangerous simply being who you are—or who other people think you are.

This is a translation of that book. In 1940, it asked Jewish children living in America to imagine what it would be like to face the challenges of life under Nazi occupation, on the eve of a war that had just begun and whose terrible course was then unforeseeable. The book called on its young readers to consider the physical, social, and moral challenges that Europe's Jews and other people in danger there faced. The book also asked its readers to think how, even though they were still children, they might understand what was happening far away from America and how they might realize its importance to their own lives—as Jews, as Americans, and as human beings.

Now, this book asks you to do the same.

J.S.

Emil and Karl

chapter one

Karl sat on a low stool, petrified. The apartment was as still as death. He looked at the pieces of the broken vase scattered on the floor. Several times he reached out with one hand to pick up an overturned chair lying beside him. The chair looked like a man who had fallen on his face and couldn't get up. But each time Karl tried, he could only lift the chair up a little bit, and then it fell down again.

It was even quieter in the kitchen and the bedroom—so quiet that he was afraid to go in there.

It wasn't that Karl minded being in the apartment by himself. He'd been left alone there more than once before; he could even go to bed by himself without being afraid. He wasn't scared of spooks or devils. Instead, he loved to stare, wide-eyed, into the darkness and make up stories.

When he went to sleep he knew that eventually he would see his mother emerge from the darkness, together with the morning. Karl didn't know where the night came from. Lying in the dark with his eyes wide open, he'd make up a story—and then suddenly he'd see his very own eyes, wide open in the light. That's how it seemed to him sometimes—that he was looking through the darkness and could see his own eyes.

But the eyes belonged to his mother, who came in with the light.

"Karl, you lazy bones, how long are you going to sleep? Get up. It's already morning. You'll be late for school."

"Mama," he whined, "Just a little more, just a little bit."

"No," his mother answered in a firm voice, but her laughing eyes made it clear that she wasn't really angry. She went straight for the blanket and uncovered his feet. The cold air felt both good and bad on his warm feet.

"Mama," he whined again, as his feet searched for the warmth of the blanket, "give me a kiss. I won't get up without one."

"It's about time a big boy like you stopped begging for kisses," his mother scolded, still pretending to be angry, and she tickled the soles of his feet.

"A kiss! A kiss!" he insisted, until he felt his mother's embrace.

No, Karl wasn't afraid to be alone, but now he

was afraid to move. He felt a chill at the thought of the narrow kitchen and the little bedroom. It was so quiet in there, much quieter than it was here by the overturned chair.

That was because just moments ago the chair had been knocked over, and the vase broken into smithereens.

It had all begun with a struggle in this room. Three big, hulking men dragged his mother away from him. Her screams could be heard outside, but no one came to help. One of the men searched their apartment, taking a few books and pamphlets, while the other two held his mother tightly.

She struggled, she spat in their faces and kept screaming, "Murderers!" Her blond hair came undone and fell in her face, covering one eye. But now her other eye seemed more powerful than both of those strong men put together. Karl could see all her strength in that one eye, blazing with rage.

The man holding the books didn't move a muscle. But then Karl bit one of the other men on the hand, making him scream with pain. Then the man with the books punched Karl in the stomach so hard that he fell down, taking the chair with him. He saw stars before his eyes. Everything went spinning around and around, and he was in so much pain that all he wanted to do was shut his eyes. But then he heard his mother screaming even louder, and that made him feel braver,

"Murderer! You hit *him*, too? Let me see my son! Aren't you going to let me say good-bye to my son?"

With her last ounce of strength she freed her left hand, which was clenched into a red fist. Quickly, like a cat, she scratched at the face of the man who was trying to restrain her, tearing his skin.

A thin trickle of blood ran down his face—then more and more, until his face was completely covered with blood. The man wiped his face with a handkerchief; Karl's mother was already on the floor where the boy lay, doubled over in pain. She kissed him quickly, trying to give him as many kisses as she could before they took her away.

"This is for tomorrow! This is for the day after tomorrow! And the day after—Karl! Karl! They're taking me away—who knows when we'll see each other again!"

Karl could taste the tears that streamed down her face.

The two men grabbed her even more roughly than before and shoved her toward the door. As they dragged her away, the vase fell from the cupboard, and pieces of it flew all over the house. One piece hit Karl in the face.

The two men held their hands over his mother's mouth, but he could still hear her screaming in a muffled voice, "Karl! Karl!"

The third man, the one who had the books and pamphlets, kicked Karl's leg and said, "Just wait, you little bastard, until we come for you."

Suddenly it seemed to Karl that the stillness in the kitchen and the bedroom was more frightening than anything else. Even if he were to stay where he was for the rest of day, and the next day, and the day after that, everything in the house would still be quiet—because his mother, his beautiful mother, would no longer be there.

That's why he lifted up the overturned chair and let it fall back down again—because it had been a part of his mother's struggle, and the pieces of the broken vase reminded him that she had only just been there, showering him with her tears.

"Karl!"

He heard someone call him, and he shivered with fear. Someone was right there in the apartment, but he was afraid to lift his head.

"Karl! Are you hungry?"

He realized it was the voice of one of their neighbors. He looked up and saw old Frau Gutenglass. Her eyes were red; she looked terrified. As she waited for him to answer, she kept glancing back at the door, which she had left open.

"No." He answered very quietly, because her fearfulness made him feel scared.

"Come into our home!"

"No," he whispered again and touched the overturned chair.

"Is my mother ever going to come back?" he asked Frau Gutenglass suddenly, in a loud voice. That's what he wanted to ask her—not *when* she was coming back. He wanted her to give him an answer. But Frau Gutenglass began to weep quietly, and she ran out of the house, shutting the door behind her.

And then Karl remembered what the man who took the books had said to him—"Just wait, you little bastard, until we come for you."

He jumped up from the stool.

It was time to run away.

"But where?" he wondered.

Run away! He stamped his foot, which is what he always did whenever he was angry or wanted to get his way with his mother.

"Karl! No more stamping your feet. It's terrible!"

Run away! He stamped his foot again—this time deliberately—and ran into the kitchen.

It was eerily quiet in the kitchen, just as he had

imagined, and in the little bedroom the silence was truly terrifying. He opened the closet and smelled the familiar fragrance of his mother's clothes. There was her coat with its fur collar, which tickled his face when she came home from work and bent over to see if he had gotten dirty while playing with his friends outside. There was her yellow hat, which looked like a huge flower in full bloom. She wore it tilted to one side, so that it showed off her hair. And there was his mother's robe, with the beautiful scent of her lilac perfume—just like lilacs in bloom, only warmer.

A pair of red slippers lay beside the bed, along with a pair of black shoes with high heels, standing up on their own. It's so nice in here, Karl thought, as he lifted up one of the slippers. Then he put it back, even with the other one, so that they would be ready. He often saw how his mother stuck her feet out of bed and slid them right into her slippers.

Suddenly he remembered that earlier he had been eating an apple. Where was it? In the kitchen. He'd taken it as he walked through the kitchen, but he couldn't remember exactly when. All he remembered was that he'd been munching away on it and got little pieces of apple peel all over the room.

"Karl, how many times have I told you not to do that?

Your mother works hard all day long, and now she has to follow after you and pick up all the little bits of apple peel that you've spat out."

He felt a pang of sadness, realizing that now he could go around and spit out as much apple peel as his heart desired, and no one would be there to scold him.

Karl bent over, and, for the first time, he began to cry. He wept quietly as he picked up the pieces of apple peel from the floor. He picked up one piece that had fallen right on the toe of his shoe. He spat lightly on the shoe and polished it with his sleeve. Then he carefully disposed of the bits of peel in a paper bag that stood near the kitchen.

It's time to run away from here.

But where? To Emil's. Yes. Go see Emil, that's the best thing to do.

Even though he opened the door without making a sound, Frau Gutenglass heard it right away. She cracked open her door, timidly poking her head out and whispering, "Karl! Where are you going? Are you hungry?"

Her kind old face pleaded with him, and he was sorry that he felt he couldn't tell her his secret—that he was running off to Emil's. No one must know.

"No, Frau Gutenglass, I'm not hungry," he

answered cautiously, so as not to let her know where he was going.

They heard steps coming from the ground floor. Frau Gutenglass slammed her door shut.

Karl ran all the way down the stairs in one breath.

chapter two

It was a cloudy day. The sky threatened to rain. It was almost spring, but the weather was cold and damp, as though it were late autumn, right before the start of winter.

Karl ran out of the building wearing a light jacket, and the cold went right through him. Even though he had just turned nine, he already knew how to take care of himself very well. Since his mother went to work, he had learned to do everything that she told him. And because he did exactly as he was told, he eventually escaped the watchful eyes of the women in the neighborhood.

Of course, Karl knew full well that he could catch a cold; still, he didn't want to go back upstairs to put on his heavy coat. Someone could be coming to get him, and he might arrive just at the same time. Perhaps it would be the same man, the one who had punched him in the stomach.

Anyway, Karl knew that he would only have to

run for a few blocks, then go up to the fourth floor of a dark building, and he would be at Emil's.

Karl hadn't seen his friend for two weeks. Emil was in his class but had stopped coming to school. On the first two days that Emil was absent Karl visited him faithfully, but then Emil's mother asked him not to come over any more.

"You mustn't, Karl, do you understand, you're not allowed to play with Emil. It will only make trouble for us. You're a sensible boy, Karl, please, don't come here any more, try to understand."

That's what Emil's mother had said to him. But Karl didn't want to be separated from his friend, and he talked about it with his own mother. She told him that he could do what he wanted. She explained that Vienna wasn't the same city that it used to be, but that things wouldn't be like this for long, because it couldn't last. Emil was a Jew, and lately things were much worse for Jews than they were for other people. Jews were being beaten, they were robbed, and their children weren't allowed to play with the others.

"But you, Karl, you can do what you want. I can't order you not to play with Emil, just as I can't force you to go ahead and play with him."

Karl told his mother that the children in school teased him about Emil, they hit him, and they even threatened to kill him if he wouldn't stop being friends with Emil.

"You see, that's what it's come to, Karl," his mother said. "You get hit because of Emil."

"Emil's my friend, and I want to play with him," Karl said, stamping his foot, as he always did when he decided to do something.

"Since you've already made up your mind, let me tell you that's just what your father would have done." His mother's eyes became teary. "And I would do the same as well."

Whenever Karl was reminded of his father, a strange feeling came over him. His father! He had barely known him. His father had died more than five years ago. Karl knew that his father had fallen while fighting for the workingman, in the bloodbath started by Hitler.

"Bloodbath . . ." "Hitler . . ." He didn't remember exactly where he'd heard these words, but they were engraved in his memory. His father died a hero—he knew that, too. But what's a hero? Karl knew the answer to that from his father's photograph, which hung in the bedroom: a tall, thin man with unusually long hands, smiling eyes, and closely cropped hair. He looked very young, and as Karl grew up, his father looked more like the boy's older brother than his father.

Whenever someone mentioned his father, Karl froze. But this soon passed, and then a warm feeling pulsed through him, the way he usually felt for someone alive.

It was enough for Karl to hear that his father would have acted the same way. That must have been what had brought him back to see Emil. But then Emil's mother wouldn't even let him in the door. Again she pleaded with him not to come back, because the neighbors were making their lives unbearable.

"It's better not to, Karl. You'll have to wait, maybe things will get better."

Emil stood at the door and pleaded with him. "I get beat up because we play together," he explained to Karl with a tremble in his voice, hoping his friend would not be insulted. "It's even worse when I go out in the street."

"Don't be angry, Karl. Your mother will understand," Emil's mother had told him.

Karl started to walk slowly. He was already very close to the building where Emil lived—but what if Emil's mother still wouldn't let him in? He walked around the block a few times. The thought almost stopped his heart from beating.

But they'd have to let him in now. He didn't have anyone else. Now he was a Jew, too. After all, he'd been punched in the stomach so hard that he could have died. They took his mother away from him. He was all alone in the world. How could Emil not let him in now?

But Karl still didn't have the courage to go up the stairs. He was terrified by the idea that they might shut the door and leave him standing outside once more. Karl decided to wait until he felt less afraid. He walked past their building one more time.

Then Karl got very upset, because he realized that he hadn't brought his father's picture with him. He became even more upset when he realized he had been in such a hurry that he hadn't even taken one last look at it. That was much worse than not bringing his coat. Soon one of the men who had taken his mother away would show up and go through their house. He would take away everything, even the picture of Karl's father.

A boy was rolling a small barrel down the street. Where did he find that beat-up old barrel? Karl wondered. The postman, with his thick, gray whiskers, walked by slowly, so slowly, as if he were moving backward. It was the same postman who went past Karl's house twice a day. Another boy, someone he knew, ran by, shouting "Hey, Karl!" Then he saw a man hammering a piece of iron—it wasn't clear to Karl what it was—banging on it harder and harder in a wild rage, as though the metal made him angry for forcing him to work.

The first boy came running back, rolling his

barrel, which had lost one of its hoops and was about to collapse.

"*Vienna isn't the same city that it used to be,*" he remembered his mother saying. He looked around to see what had changed. The postman was still walking backwards.

Then Karl remembered his great secret. It was so special and so secret that he wasn't even allowed to tell his mother. That's what his teacher had made him promise when she told it to him—never to tell anyone, not a single soul.

It had been during those first days, when everything started to change for the worse. Their teacher suddenly changed the way she spoke and began saying all kinds of strange, wild things. She was an older woman, with a calm manner and a gentle, peaceful voice. She would never get upset; she'd smile even when the whole class misbehaved.

But best of all was the beautiful way that she spoke. Karl, who liked to make up his own stories, loved to listen to her melodious voice. Even when her students didn't understand what the words meant, her voice went straight to their hearts. Karl loved to think up stories and imagine how they would sound in her musical voice.

Then, suddenly, their teacher changed. She became nervous and angry, she shouted, things fell from her hands—the same teacher who used to act so kindly and calmly. She also began singing new kinds of songs with her class in a shrill voice. She had become a completely different person.

The children picked on Emil. They would wait around for him when he came to school or at lunchtime. Before he could escape, Emil would find himself surrounded. They'd circle around him, taunting him with nasty songs. As they got rowdier, they'd spit in his face and even hit him. They'd pretend to open up the circle a little bit, but as soon as Emil tried to escape they'd close in on him again. So Emil would stand in the middle like a frightened little bird and cry.

Once, though, Emil didn't cry. He just shouted, "Shame! Shame on you!" But the children weren't ashamed at all; they only attacked him more fiercely. Still, Emil refused to cry. Instead, he responded stubbornly each time they hit him: "Shame on you! Shame!"

Karl usually sat off to one side. He would pretend that he had a gun and could get rid of them all. Then he could grab Emil by the hand and rescue him. But this time Karl's imaginary gun wasn't enough. His throat felt tight, as though something was stuck in there. Karl leaped up, broke through the crowd, and stood next to Emil:

"Stop hitting him, stop picking on him!"

He stood in front of Emil, protecting him with his broad back. Emil just kept shouting like a madman, in a hoarse, mechanical voice, "Shame on you! Shame!"

The circle closed again, and the children pranced around the two of them. They stopped trying to hit Emil but kept on singing their hateful songs.

Just then their teacher was passing through the schoolyard. She stopped and stood there, motionless.

"My God," she said, raising her hand to her head. "What is this?"

"We were beating up Emil, he's just a filthy Jew, and now Karl's taking his side," the children squealed.

The circle opened up, but Karl and Emil stayed where they were.

"And why are you hitting Emil?" The teacher asked them softly.

"Why are we hitting him?! Everyone beats up Jews nowadays. Emil's a Jew, he's not our equal."

The boy who spoke was the tallest in the class. He always scowled and walked with a limp. Sometimes when the others fought with him they would kick his lame foot on purpose. But now he was their leader, and he showed the others that he was as good as they were.

"We're just practicing on Emil, so we can take care of grown-up Jews when we're bigger," he said, as he hopped over to the teacher, limping on his bad foot. "And we're going to tell that you're on the side of a lousy Jew."

Some of the children had backed off from the circle. Perhaps they felt a little sorry for what they had done. But when they saw how boldly the boy with the limp threatened their teacher, they stepped forward again and started shouting.

Everyone turned to look at Emil, who was hiding behind Karl.

"I'll show you what to do. Then, when you're grown up, you'll already know," the teacher said. She was trying to speak with her former gentleness, but her voice sounded different. "I'm not on Emil's side. Emil is an inferior being."

"Hurray!" the children roared, "That's the right idea."

"Emil is a common Jew. Aryan children shouldn't dirty their hands with such filth," the teacher continued.

"Hurray!" they all screamed, and each one of the children ran past Emil and spat on him, calling out, "Dirty Jew! Dirty Jew!"

All the while, Karl stood by Emil, and when the teacher saw that Karl hadn't budged, she said to him, "And you, Karl, I want to see you. I want to show you what it means to interfere with pure Aryan children."

A short while later, Karl was standing in the classroom. The teacher sat down and held her forehead with her bony hand, covering her eyes.

"Karl, are we alone?"

"Yes," he stammered.

"Are you positive that no one else is in the room?"

"I'm sure," Karl said, frightened, as he heard her speak with her former tenderness.

"Karl, swear to me by God that you won't tell anyone what I am going to tell you."

"No one," he mumbled.

"Not even your mother?"

Karl lifted his large blue eyes and looked at her.

"Yes, not even your mother. This is a special secret, just between the two of us."

Karl felt very honored that his teacher trusted him with such an important secret, and he promised not to tell anyone, not even his mother.

"Karl, I have to speak to you, because I can't talk to anyone about this. Your father died a hero. His blood was shed for us."

Karl stood erect, trying to show respect for his father's memory.

"Someday, when you're grown up, you'll think about me. By then I'll be long dead. I'm old, Karl.

"What will you think of me?" the teacher continued, taking her hand away from her eyes. She looked straight at Karl's face, as if she wanted to know what he would think of her then.

"My God, I get a chill when I think about it. You protected poor Emil with your own body, and I insulted him horribly."

Karl came a little closer to the teacher, because now she was speaking so softly that he could barely hear her.

"I'm already old and broken, I have no more strength. I don't have the strength to stand up against everyone and fight, to spit in their faces—forgive me, Karl, but I can't. Someday you will pass judgment on me. People such as you will judge me; please be merciful."

She took his hand, and he felt how her cold hand trembled.

"I've been ordered to teach them how to hate, to make Jews the scapegoat, but what can I teach them, these youngsters, these vulgar children? They're teaching me, they're already completely corrupt. They think up the wildest things. I could learn from them how to be evil. Children need to be taught good, but evil? You saw it yourself, Karl."

Now she spoke just like the teacher that she used to be. Her words had their familiar warmth, just like a song. You couldn't forget words like that, even if you didn't understand them.

"I've already seen to it that Emil no longer has to come to school; he needn't suffer any more. Even this was difficult to do. I've had to lie, to pretend, because they, the Aryans, must have their scapegoat."

She got up and began walking around the classroom. Then she came right up to Karl, almost whispering into his ear.

"And you, you must protect your precious heart. Our unfortunate country needs it. That little bit of decency is our only hope. Be good to Emil, protect him whenever you can. Perhaps someday we adults will be ashamed of what we've done."

The teacher heard a knock at the door. Her whole body trembled. Suddenly she began to shout, "You swine, you swine, you must understand the difference between yourself and the Jews."

A gang of children burst into the room.

The teacher shouted at the top of her voice, "You little swine!"

The change took Karl by surprise.

He was frightened and took a step back, but then he remembered the special promise he had made. A warm feeling went through him, and once again his throat felt tight. He couldn't keep it in any longer—he began to cry.

The boy with the limp started to chant, and the other children joined in:

"Karl's a swine! Karl's a swine! Let's hear it for our teacher!"

For the seventh time, Karl stood before the building where Emil lived. From the cloudy sky a few raindrops fell, so few that he could count them. It was getting dark. Karl shivered in his light jacket, and he felt hunger pangs deep in his stomach.

He looked around, then walked into the building and scrambled up the dark, steep staircase.

He gave three short knocks and then three long knocks on the door. That was the special signal he and Emil used.

chapter three

The door opened, and Emil stood there, looking dazed. He didn't say a word. He just stood in the open doorway, not knowing what to do. Karl could tell that his friend felt ill at ease, and so he didn't dare go inside. They both stood there and stared at each other.

Emil was usually much more fidgety than Karl, but now he was as still as a statue. He usually spoke quickly, talking about everything at once so fast that he tripped over his words, and as he spoke he couldn't stay in one place. His whole body talked— his eyes, his head, his hands, his feet. But now he stood as still as stone.

"The rabbi is here," Emil said, as he began to come alive. "We've had a terrible disaster." His long face seemed quite drawn as he lowered his eyes.

As Emil held the door open, Karl thought it made sense that Emil had said the word "disaster." All day long he had been looking for the right word, and "disaster" described what he had been through as well.

"I've had a terrible disaster, too," Karl said.

Then Emil started talking quickly. He let go of the door, and it swung shut, but Karl caught hold of it and held it open.

"They came," Emil explained, "in the middle of the night and woke up everybody in the house. They beat my father and took him away. Then they killed him, and they cremated him, and they sent the ashes back to us in a box. And yesterday was the funeral. I was there, and my mother and the rabbi and Uncle Robert. Nobody else."

Karl shivered and said softly, "They took my mother away from me. Three men came today and dragged her off. And she scratched one of them but good," he said proudly.

Hearing this, Emil took hold of the door and motioned Karl inside.

Emil's mother sat in the middle of the room on a small footstool. She looked older than Karl's mother. Her hair was half black, half white. She didn't even notice that Karl had come in. Every so often she broke into tears, but right away she put her hand over her mouth, as if to stifle her crying. She managed to stop, but only for a while. Soon she broke into sobs once more.

The rabbi stood by the window, drumming his fingers lightly on the glass. He was a middle-aged man with a short blond beard trimmed to a point. In one hand he held his eyeglasses, which he had just removed. His eyes were wet with tears. Each time that Emil's mother started to cry, the rabbi went over to her and put his hands on her shoulders. He started to speak in a broken voice, but right away he recovered and spoke clearly.

"You mustn't, you mustn't let so much sadness into your heart. The living must continue to live, in spite of their enemies." When he thought that his words had comforted her somewhat, the rabbi returned to the dark window.

Now Karl wished that he hadn't come to Emil's. He couldn't find a place for himself there. He wished that Emil's mother would get up from her footstool and tell him to leave. But she didn't even see him.

The rabbi put his glasses back on. He went over to Emil and said, "Be a good boy." And he added in a softer voice, "Take care of your mother. I'll come back tomorrow." Then the rabbi noticed Karl for the first time. He asked Emil, "Who is this boy—a friend of yours?"

"They took his mother away," Emil quickly stammered. He wanted to defend Karl, to explain why he was there. "And his father died a long time ago."

"May God have mercy on us," the rabbi said and quickly left.

As soon as the rabbi had gone, Emil's mother got up from her footstool. Emil wanted her to see that Karl was there.

"They took away his—" Emil started to explain.

"I know. I heard, my son, I heard," his mother interrupted. "Children, are you hungry?"

"Yes," Karl cried out. Then he noticed that she was walking about in stocking feet. He felt bad that he had shouted "Yes" so loudly, but he felt such sharp, stabbing pains in his stomach.

"I'm hungry, very hungry," he cried again, and looked about for something to eat.

Emil's mother cut some slices of bread, spread them with butter, and put some cheese on top. Karl grabbed his sandwich and devoured it at once.

After a while the two boys lay in bed. The room they slept in was pitch black, as was the other room of the apartment. But in there was a glass sitting on a bureau, a glass with a burning wick inside. The flame flickered in a mirror on the opposite wall. The dancing wick sputtered and crackled, as if it were about to go out, but then the flame came back right away and trembled as it continued to burn. From the bed Karl could see Emil's mother, still sitting on the low stool.

"Karl, are you asleep?"

"No."

"Do you know why they killed my father?"

"No," Karl answered quietly.

"Don't you know? It's because we're Jews . . . Karl?" Emil asked. "Are you scared?"

"No! Are you?"

"Yes. I'm scared of the candle in the other room. It's for my father's soul."

"Emil, are you sleeping?"

"No. Karl, are you afraid now, too?"

"No. I was thinking . . . "

"What about?"

"About our teacher . . . "

"What about her?"

"Nothing . . . "

Karl remembered that he had sworn not to tell.

"Karl, are your eyes open?"

"Yes, Emil."

"I'm keeping mine shut tight—so tight that it hurts . . . "

"Emil, why did they take my mother away?" Karl suddenly asked, very quietly.

Emil didn't respond. Karl liked that his friend didn't have an answer for him immediately. Usually Emil had an answer for everything, but this time Karl had asked him something hard.

"Well, why did they kill my father?" Karl asked. He was teasing Emil for not knowing the answer, but this gave Emil a clue.

"Your father was a Socialist. Everybody knows that. My father always said that your father was on the side of the poor workingman. And your mother is also a Socialist."

"Are they going to cremate my mother, too?" Karl asked.

Emil didn't answer.

"Emil, are you asleep?"

"No! I'm too scared. Come over here . . . " Karl moved nearer, but he kept one eye on the other room, where the little flame cast everything in shadow. He saw Emil's mother was still sitting there. He couldn't see the little stool any longer, so it seemed as though she was sitting on the floor.

Suddenly, they heard her sobbing. The sound rose up from the floor. It was more muffled than before, but it lasted longer.

"Emil, are you asleep?" Karl asked softly.

He lay in bed with his eyes open and stared into the darkness, until he saw Emil sit up in bed, holding his head with both hands. By then it was morning, and they could see through the window that it was raining heavily outside.

chapter four

Even though he was still under the covers, Karl began to shiver from the cold. He also noticed that Emil's mother was still sitting on the little footstool.

"Had she been sitting like that all night long?" he asked himself, frightened.

He wanted to ask Emil—but with his head buried in his hands, Emil suddenly looked like an old man. Karl was afraid to look at him.

At first, Karl pretended to be asleep. He rolled over on his side and closed his eyes. He wished he could fall asleep, and then, when he woke up, everything would be better. Emil's mother wouldn't still be sitting there, and Emil wouldn't look like an old man—that's what Karl tried to convince himself.

But he couldn't keep his eyes shut for long, because even then he could still see Emil. Karl began tossing from side to side, trying to make a commotion. Sure enough, the bed squeaked. That's good, Karl thought, and he opened his eyes to see if Emil's mother had moved even a little bit. No, she was still sitting in the same place.

The rain made a terrible racket. The heavy drops hit the window like hail. He could hear water splashing onto the stones in the courtyard, as if it was running from a pipe.

"You know, Karl," Emil said, without moving—as though he'd known all along that his friend wasn't asleep—"I'm afraid to get out of bed."

"Have you been up long?" Karl asked.

"Yes, for a long time. I called to my mother, but she didn't answer."

"You didn't shout loud enough, Emil," Karl assured him. "You were probably afraid of waking me up."

Emil took his friend's advice. He called out, "Mama!" When she didn't respond, he shouted louder and louder, "Mama! Mama! Mama!"

After the last shout Karl heard his friend crying. But this time he didn't have anything reassuring to say to Emil. It was all so strange. Emil's mother was sitting on the little stool and hadn't moved one bit.

Karl jumped out of bed and quickly threw on his clothes. He felt he had to do something. Taking firm steps, he walked into the room where Emil's mother sat.

As soon as he entered, a chill ran through his body. She sat there with her head bent over. Even though he took such heavy steps that they made the bureau shake, she didn't move.

Then Emil got up the courage to jump out of bed. Still in his underwear, he ran in and stood in front of his mother.

"Mama! Mama!"

He waited for a while, but she still just stared at the floor.

"Mama! Answer me, Mama! I'm frightened! Mama, you're scaring me!"

All at once he started to cry and grabbed his mother's shoulders.

Strangely enough, as soon as he started to cry, her body began to move, and she looked up from the floor. She looked at him for a moment or two, her eyes brimming with tears. It seemed as though she yearned to say something—not with her mouth, but with her eyes. Her face was full of kindness, but her mouth remained closed, and soon her gaze dropped to the floor once more.

Emil went over to the table and banged it with his fist in desperation.

"Mama, you're frightening me! Why won't you answer me?"

Once again his mother didn't respond until Emil shouted at her. Then, as soon as he began to cry, she lifted her teary eyes and looked at him with her quiet, loving face.

Karl saw right away that Emil's mother had changed overnight. He felt that now Emil was even more helpless than he was, and that he had to do something to help his friend.

Karl thought of his neighbor, Frau Gutenglass, who was always so kind to him and his mother.

"We ought to go to a neighbor," he said, because often when his mother had gone to work that's what he'd have to do.

"No, God forbid!" Emil cried. "Anything's better than the neighbors!"

Emil told him how their neighbor across the hall had helped beat up his father. The man's wife had also been there the day before, and she took away almost all of his mother's clothes. She even held them up to her body as she looked in the mirror and said that they were just right for her.

"But we have to do something, Emil, we can't just let things stay the way they are."

As Emil and Karl continued to talk, Emil's mother still sat there, motionless. Neither of the boys could take his eyes off her, hoping that they might see some change.

The rain continued to fall, though not as heavily. Now it was a thin, steady drizzle.

"Maybe we should go find your Uncle Robert," Karl suggested.

"No, never! Uncle Robert warned us not to come to see him. They looted his store. It's dangerous to walk down his street. They beat up anyone they find there. I'm too scared to go outside."

Karl wanted to ask who exactly "they" were, but suddenly he remembered the three men who had dragged off his mother.

There was a clock on the wall in Emil's house, but it had stopped. "It must be about twelve o'clock by now," Emil said, when he saw Karl looking at the clock.

"How do you know?"

"Because I'm very hungry," Emil answered.

Karl was, too, but he was ashamed to admit it.

Suddenly Emil went over to his friend.

"Karl, you won't leave me alone, will you?"

"What are you thinking? Where would I go? I don't have anyone else."

"What about your grandmother?"

"No, she's very old and sick. She's in a hospital. I don't even know where it is."

"You know, maybe we'll have to take my mother to a hospital," Emil said.

Emil was still afraid that Karl would abandon him, so he tried to see if he could be sure of his friend.

"You know, Karl, if you walk out of here no one's going to hit you. After all, you're not a Jew."

"Well, they kicked me, they beat up my mother," Karl responded.

Emil was satisfied. He found some bread and gave it to Karl.

Karl didn't want to take it at first, but then he bit off some.

Emil also broke off a piece and chewed on it half-heartedly.

Karl could tell that Emil was very frightened. He went over to Emil and took his hand.

"Emil, you're the only friend I have."

Emil's eyes began to fill with tears.

"The only one," Karl reassured him.

Once more Emil went over to his mother, but now he was less afraid than before. He didn't shout desperately as he had earlier, but whispered into her ear.

"Mama, why won't you say anything?"

They heard someone knock softly on the door. The boys froze. Slowly, cautiously, the door opened, and the rabbi walked in.

chapter five

The rabbi didn't waste a minute. As soon as he saw the condition that Emil's mother was in, he left the house. He came back quickly with two other men. One of them went right over to where she was sitting. He examined her for a while and then shook his head, looking at the rabbi sadly.

"Yes, Rabbi," he said, "It's most unfortunate. We'll have to take her away at once."

"God," said the rabbi, making a fist. "Why are You silent in the face of these wicked men? God, how long, how long?"

He dropped into a chair and ran his fingers through his hair several times, as though he wanted to tear it out by the roots.

"We're all losing our minds, Doctor. This is the third case like this that I've seen today. Merciful God, what do You want from us? Why have You turned away from us?"

Although it seemed that he spoke without any

feeling, tears streamed from behind his glasses and ran down his face. But the rabbi made no attempt to wipe the tears away.

The two other men stood beside Emil's mother, their heads bowed. Emil and Karl grasped each other by the hand. Emil squeezed Karl's hand so hard that he almost cried out in pain.

The two men helped Emil's mother up from her footstool. She didn't resist at all. They helped her into her coat, because all at once she started to shiver.

As she walked between the two men, her face lit up with a smile. She took in the entire room with her warm eyes. She stopped in front of Emil, but only his lips moved.

"Mama, Mama!"

Her face glowed as she stood in front of her son. She opened her mouth as though she wanted to respond to him, but she made no sound. Then her smile changed into a grimace of pain. All her tenderness vanished. Her body stretched upward, so that she seemed taller than she really was. Her face looked strained to the point of bursting, and then she let out a scream.

The wick that had been burning all night flickered for the last time and went out. The strong smell of molten wax filled the room.

As soon as the scream escaped from her, Emil's mother seemed calmer. Her entire body trembled with cold; even her teeth were chattering. The two men led her out of the house.

The rabbi tried to get up from his chair but sank back into it. He remained seated for a few minutes, then got up and walked to the door with shaky steps.

But Emil broke away from Karl and ran toward the door, blocking the rabbi's path.

"What will happen to me—to us?"

His voice sounded hoarse, almost like an adult's. His face looked frightened and angry.

"What's going to happen to us?" he screamed.

"I'm sorry, Emil, forgive me. I almost forgot about you," he said, stroking the boy's head. "A great tragedy has befallen us all. There are hundreds now, just like you, just like him," he said, pointing to Karl. "Yes, hundreds. Little children, without any parents."

He stroked the boy's hair and face but avoided looking at him.

"I'm leaving now, but I'll come back later. We're looking for a home for children like you, a home where you can get something warm to eat and have a place to sleep."

"For Karl, too?" Emil asked.

"Certainly, certainly, for him, too. We won't abandon him, just as we pray that God won't abandon us."

And so the hours passed. Emil and Karl waited, their hearts pounding. They barely spoke to each other, but listened for the faintest noise—footsteps, perhaps, or a knock at the door. But there was still no sign of the rabbi.

Darkness had fallen, and Emil huddled close to Karl.

"Are you scared?" Emil asked.

"Yes," he answered firmly. "Now I'm really scared."

"It doesn't look like the rabbi will come."

"No, it doesn't look like the rabbi will come," Karl repeated.

"Maybe someone beat him up," said Karl, thinking it over.

"Yes, maybe," Emil answered.

"Come with me," said Karl, taking him by the hand. "Come on, we have to run away from this place before it gets really dark."

"But where will we go?"

Karl pulled him along forcefully.

At the door Karl remembered something.

"Put on your coat, it's cold outside," he ordered Emil, in the same tone that his mother would use.

Emil put on his coat.

"Maybe you have another coat for me?" Karl asked.

Emil rummaged through the closet and took out something. Karl tried it on, but it was so tight on him that it almost tore.

"Too bad, I'll just have to go like this," said Karl, opening the door.

Karl ran quickly down the steps, with Emil behind him. Once they were outside, they just stood there like two frightened puppies. Karl began to creep along the wall, pulling Emil after him.

"Let's go back to my building. Frau Gutenglass wanted to take me in and give me a place to sleep and something to eat. She's very nice, I'm sure she'll take care of you, too."

Karl walked toward the apartment house that he had fled only the day before. He walked up the few flights to what had been his home, but now he was afraid even to look at the door. Instead he went straight to his neighbor's door and knocked on it hesitantly.

The door remained shut. Karl waited a while and then knocked again. He started to shout, "Frau Gutenglass! Frau Gutenglass!"

Karl knocked and then pushed the door, and it opened all by itself. He stood there, trembling.

Even though it was dark, Karl could see that no one was home. He went in and began to walk from one room to the next. He knew every corner of the place well. But now it all seemed strange and unfamiliar, because the apartment was empty.

There wasn't a piece of furniture left except in the kitchen, where a large table still stood. He remembered it well, having sat there eating with Frau Gutenglass and her husband, who used to tell him lots of funny stories.

But now the emptiness of the rooms seemed so strange that he couldn't believe his eyes. He went out to the hall and looked at the brass plate on the door.

"Yes, that's right." It said "JAKOB GUTENGLASS," with the "G" rubbed off so that it looked as though it said "UTENGLASS."

He felt embarrassed in front of Emil. He felt as though he had misled his friend, and now he had no idea what to do.

"You know," he said to Emil, "It's too bad the rabbi didn't come back.

"Just yesterday Frau Gutenglass was living here," Karl explained, "and she asked me to come in. I'm sure that she was still living here. See, the name's on the door. And we lived across from them, over here. You can still see our name."

But Karl still didn't want to turn around and look at his own door.

As both of them began to walk slowly down the stairs, a door opened on the second floor.

"Karl!" Karl recognized one of his neighbors. Karl was glad to see him and started to say something.

"Shh . . . Karl. Here, take this." The neighbor quickly handed him a package and shut the door.

It smelled like roasted meat. Without saying a word, Karl and Emil began to devour the food. They finished everything that was in the package—the bread, the potatoes, and the meat. They ate so fast that when they were finished they could barely catch their breath.

"That sure was tasty!" Emil stammered. Then they threw away the greasy piece of paper that was left.

Night had already fallen when they walked out of the building. Emil and Karl stood there and looked at each other. Karl waited for Emil to suggest something, but Emil had no idea of what to say. He was waiting for his friend to come up with something.

Suddenly they both ran back into the building. Karl forgot to grab hold of Emil's hand, but there was no need to, because Emil ran right behind him.

When they were back inside, Karl asked, his heart pounding with fear, "Did you see those two men?"

"Yes," Emil answered, panting.

"They were dressed just like the ones who took my mother away."

Emil was too frightened to speak. He tried to several times, but he couldn't.

When he calmed down, he explained to Karl that that's just how the men looked—the ones who had beaten his father the other night and taken him away, covered with blood.

"We'll have to sleep here, in the cellar," Karl decided. "And we'll have to stay there until morning."

"In the cellar?" Emil asked, trembling.

"I know every corner of it," Karl reassured him. "I even have a kitten who sleeps down there at night."

But Emil didn't budge.

"You have to stop being scared," Karl insisted and forced Emil several steps toward the cellar.

It was pitch black in the cellar. Karl tapped his way along the wall and guided Emil along behind him. He told Emil to lie down.

Emil obeyed, but he began to cry.

"They could still find us here," Karl whispered. "Be quiet, you can't make any noise."

Emil whimpered in the silence.

"Just pretend that this is an island, and we're here

all alone," Karl said to comfort him. "And when it gets light, we'll climb up the trees and eat nuts."

All at once he gave Emil a poke and exclaimed happily, "We're not alone. Did you hear that noise? That's my kitten."

"Psst—Psst—Psst," Karl called.

Soon the kitten found its way to Karl. Emil stroked its fur in the darkness, and he felt a little more at ease.

"It must be nice to be a kitten," Emil said, thinking out loud, his eyes shut.

"Shh. Don't talk, go to sleep. Good night, Emil!" Karl yawned, exhausted.

chapter six

A bit of light shone through a small window that was covered with an iron grating. The windowpane was so black that the light making its way through it looked grimy.

Emil was the first to open his eyes. He'd slept poorly all night, tossing from side to side. Several times he'd heard Karl cry out in his sleep, which terrified Emil. But now Karl was sleeping peacefully. He lay on his back, and in the dim light it seemed to Emil that his friend was smiling in his sleep.

It wasn't long before Karl woke up, too. He opened his eyes and looked at Emil as though he didn't recognize him. But as soon as Karl looked up at the little window, he realized where he was.

"I had such a nice dream," he told Emil. "Your mother and my mother were taking us to the park. We were all dressed up. We played on the seesaw, we rode on the carousel, and my father was sitting on a bench, reading a book. We ran into our teacher in the garden, and she wagged her finger at me, but then she smiled. Then, all of a sudden you and I started to run, and both of our mothers ran after us, and they were laughing. Everything was so nice, the birds were singing, the carousel was playing music."

"It must have been a nice dream. You were smiling in your sleep. But during the night you cried out, and I got scared."

Emil propped himself up on one side. It was a hard place to sleep.

Overhead they heard a scraping noise, going back and forth. They realized that someone was sweeping with a broom.

"The janitor is sweeping the steps," said Karl. "It must still be early, it must be when we usually leave for school."

Both boys lay there, not wanting to get up. Suddenly the door opened, and a short man walked over to a corner, put away a broom, and picked up two others, laying them across his shoulders as if he were carrying rifles.

Karl let out a cough, and the janitor turned around, startled. "Who's there?" He shouted, standing still.

When Karl didn't answer, the janitor came nearer, looked closely, then clapped his hands together. "Karl! Karl! What are you doing here?"

He didn't wait for an answer, but began to shout, "Berta! Berta!"

A woman with unkempt hair came running in a panic. She stood close to the boys and peered at Karl, with her small, nearsighted eyes.

"Can this be Karl?" she exclaimed.

"Yes," Karl answered, feeling happy inside, because he was with people he knew.

"Did you sleep here all night?" the janitor asked. "Was this your bed?"

"Yes," Karl answered.

"Terrible! Terrible!" the janitor shouted. He ran around in the cellar, and kept shouting, "Terrible! Terrible!"

"Hush, Josef," said his wife, trying to calm him.

"No, don't 'hush' me, I feel like shouting. Let them come and punish me, I'm not afraid. Terrible! Terrible!"

"Josef, please, be quiet," Berta pleaded.

Karl felt very grateful that the janitor was so concerned. The boy quickly explained what had happened to his friend Emil and to his father and mother.

"And how is *your* mother, have you heard anything from her?"

"No," Karl answered, lowering his head.

"Terrible! Terrible! Berta, what has happened to the world?"

The two boys sat on the floor, not moving from their places.

"Take them into the house. We have to give them something to eat."

When he saw that his wife hadn't moved, the janitor threw down the brooms and lifted up both boys.

"I'm not afraid of anyone. Let them come. I want to know if it's against the law to give food to such poor, unfortunate children. I'd like to hear it with my own ears."

And when Berta still stood there, the janitor shouted so loud at her that she trembled. "Are you no longer afraid of God?"

"Josef!" she cried in a pleading voice.

He took hold of Emil with one hand and Karl with the other and led them up several steps. There he opened a door and led the boys down a few more steps. It was dark, but then the janitor opened another door and it became lighter. He brought the boys into a cramped basement room.

This room was a little brighter than the cellar. Emil saw his reflection in a rusty mirror, and it frightened him. He was so filthy that he didn't recognize himself.

Just then the janitor's wife came over to him with a cold, wet cloth. She gave his face a good washing and then washed his hands, wiping each finger clean. Then she did the same with Karl. The boys felt somewhat refreshed by the cold cloth, which the janitor's wife rinsed out several times in a basin.

She set out bread, butter, and cheese and poured them each half a glass of milk. The boys didn't say a word; they ate in silence. The basement room was quiet. Emil looked carefully at the janitor's wife, noticing the reddish color of her hair. He also saw that the janitor didn't have any hair at all, but he had a heavy mustache that drooped over each side of his mouth.

Josef sat in the farthest corner of the room and rocked slowly in his chair. When the boys finished eating, he spoke to them.

"Every night you should come and sleep in the cellar, do you hear me, Karl? And you, what is your name?"

Karl answered for him. "His name is Emil."

"Karl, Emil—every night. I'll put something down on the floor for you to sleep on. No one will dare disturb you. No one!" he shouted, as he rose from his rocking chair.

"Josef! Josef! You'll make things bad for us all."

"I'm not afraid, let them come. Are they going to shoot at me? Let them. I'll just ask them, one man to another. I'll point to these two boys. See, this is Emil and this is Karl! Is there anything wrong with that? I'll ask them." He banged on the table. "Berta, I'm not afraid."

After this he calmed down, and he walked out of the house with slow, tired steps. He returned with the two brooms over his shoulder, like two rifles. He picked up a few rags, then took a can and shook it to see if there was still anything inside.

"There's still enough kerosene," his wife told him. Josef left the house without looking behind.

Berta went over to Karl and gave him a kiss. She kissed Emil, then took a basket and went over to the door.

"I'm going shopping for supper," she told them as she stood by the door. "Why don't you finish your milk, Karl?"

After she left, Karl told Emil that Josef and Berta were very good people. Everyone in the building liked them. Not long ago their only child, who was five years old, had died.

"My mother always used to say that the janitor has a heart of gold. He never yells at us kids. He plays with us whenever he has time."

"All the other kids must be in school by now," Emil said suddenly in a wistful voice.

Karl stood on a chair and stuck his head out the small window. "It's nice outside," he said to Emil. "What do you say, should we go out? The sun is shining, and it's not raining any more."

"But what about Josef and Berta?" asked Emil. "What will they say when they can't find us?"

"Oh, we'll come right back." He jumped down off the chair. "We'll go out for a while, just to say 'good morning' to the sun. Come on, Emil, we'll just walk up and down the street a few times, and then we'll come right back."

Emil didn't really want to go outside, but he followed his friend.

chapter seven

Emil was terrified to be outside. It was beautiful and sunny, but he kept tripping over his own feet. In fact, it was the bright light that made Emil so afraid. Karl was running, almost skipping down the street, and Emil trudged after his friend with reluctant footsteps.

Emil realized that he actually felt safer in Josef's cellar. Now the sunlight forced him to open his eyes, but he was afraid to look around.

Karl knew that Emil wasn't very happy to be out on the street. As Emil straggled along after him, Karl consoled his friend. "Look, we'll just look around for a little bit, and then we'll go back to Josef's. Josef and his wife are very good people," Karl added, to show Emil that even though he was excited to be outside he hadn't forgotten all about his friend.

Little streams of water from the previous day's rain, now warmed by the sun, ran down the pavement. Karl charged boldly down the center of the street.

"We're going too far," Emil pleaded.

"Don't worry, I can't get lost here. We'll turn here on this street, turn left on the next street, and then I'll show you a trick. We go into that big building, then through the courtyard, and we come back out on this street," said Karl, showing off his expertise.

Emil let himself be persuaded, and he began to run after Karl. He even began to feel like playing tag with his friend, when all of a sudden he caught sight of a grocery store. Though the shop was locked up behind a metal grate, all its windows had been shattered. Shards of glass were scattered in front of the store. Usually a shop window like this would be filled with all sorts of jars and cans, different kinds of bread and sausages, but now it was littered with slivers of glass, and all the display stands had been stripped bare.

Emil stood there, trembling. Karl sensed that something had happened to his friend. He, too, came to a halt, looked at the shop, and all at once his happy mood vanished. He stood frozen in place.

"Look," said Karl, pointing at another store. According to its sign, it was a shoe store. It had been left wide open. The windows on both sides had been knocked out completely. The display window was empty, and inside dozens of open boxes lay scattered about. Between the grocery and a clothing store was yet another store, a butcher shop, which stood undisturbed, open for business. The butcher, wearing a bloodstained apron, stood calmly in the doorway. There was no one in his shop, so he walked slowly over to the shoe store and looked in, folding his arms and tucking in his hands, as if to warm them up. He bent over and took a long look inside. Then he walked over to the grocery and examined its empty window. He picked up a couple of pieces of glass and tossed them into the street. Then the butcher sat down on a bench in front of his store, took out a cigarette, and lit it. All at once he burst out laughing. He laughed so hard that he almost choked on the smoke.

"Let's go back," Emil pleaded.

"Sure, we're going back," Karl replied, but he couldn't tear his eyes away from the two shops with their shattered, empty windows.

As they started to walk away, a man appeared from a side street. He was dressed in the same kind of uniform as the men Emil and Karl had seen the night before, which had sent them racing into the cellar.

But now it was too late to run away. They both froze in their places. Neither one made the slightest attempt to escape.

"And what are you boys doing out in the street

at this time of day?" the stranger asked, grabbing Emil's shoulder. "Why aren't you in school?"

Both boys stood there, their heads bowed.

"Why aren't you in school?" The man in the uniform shouted so loudly that it startled the butcher, and he jumped up from his seat.

"Because, because—" Emil stammered, "Because I'm a Jew."

Emil began to cry, and the man, who was holding onto him as though he were a criminal, wasn't entirely sure that he'd heard correctly.

"Why?" he asked again.

"Because I'm a Jew," Emil answered through his tears.

"Is that so!" the man stretched his body to its full height. "A little Jewboy, just as I suspected!"

The butcher, still in his bloody apron, came closer.

The man in the uniform waited patiently as the butcher approached. And when the butcher looked at him and began to smile, the man in the uniform raised his foot and kicked the butcher so hard that he fell over. The butcher got right up and ran back to his bench, and he sat down.

From the bench the butcher began to shout, "You have no right to beat up your fellow man, no right. No, none whatsoever!"

The man in the uniform turned to Karl. "And

you, what are you, a Jewboy, too?"

"A friend of his," Karl answered quietly.

A slap rang out, and Karl fell down. When he got up, a warm stream of blood gushed from his nose. He tried to stop it with his hands, and they became completely covered with blood.

Emil cried even louder when he saw the blood running from Karl's nose.

"Come on, Jewboy, and you, too, Jewboy's friend," the man said, and he began to herd them along.

"Stop crying," Karl said quietly to Emil.

Even though the boys didn't resist, the man in the uniform dragged them along roughly, as if they were about to break away and run off.

He took them into an alley, where there wasn't another living soul to be seen. Suddenly a short, stout woman came out of a house. She stood there, using her body to block the path of the man, who was still dragging Emil and Karl.

The woman clasped her hands together. "Now you let go of those two boys, Rudolf, do you hear me, my great big hero? Otherwise, dear husband of mine, I'll split your head open."

"Leave me alone, duty is duty."

"I'll give you 'duty,' my fine hero. How much beer have you poured down your throat? What d'you want with these two?"

He tried to continue on his way, but she stood there like a wall and wouldn't let him pass.

"These are Jewboys!"

"Kids are kids, my big hero," and she spat right in his face.

"I'll have to arrest you," he yelled, "I'll tell the authorities. I do my duty, and a wife's not supposed to interfere." He gripped Emil and Karl so tightly that he almost pulled off their skin.

The woman cleared the path for him and let him pass by. "Go on, go on, my fine hero, do your duty, but I'm warning you! Don't you dare come home. I'll split your head open."

She started to walk away but then came running back. "Rudolf, wait! What'll you do with those two?"

He grabbed Emil and Karl with his left hand, clicked his boots together and saluted with his right hand. "It's my duty. *Heil!*"

The woman turned and hurried away, as if she wanted to escape. But as she ran, she shouted down the length of the entire street. "You drunkard, let go of them! Listen to me, let them go!"

chapter eight

As soon as they left the narrow alley, the bright sun blinded them. It seemed to Emil as though someone had taken a huge mirror and turned it so that the sun was shining right into their eyes. He stood there, dazed. The man who had been holding onto the boys gripped them even firmer. He also stopped in his tracks, surprised by the bright sun.

Before Karl got used to the light, it looked as if there was a river in front of them, with hundreds of people swimming in it. At first the boys were spellbound by what they saw. Karl was so curious that he tried to run over and see what was happening, but the man held him back. Emil was curious, too, but he was too frightened to move closer. If the man had let go of them, Emil would have simply run away without even turning around.

They had never seen anything like it in their lives—not on a Sunday or even a holiday. They were standing near a large public square. Hundreds of people were there, some of them down on the ground, others running back and forth. There was a great commotion, with lots of shouting. As Karl watched, his eyes grew wider and wider.

The closer they came to the people on the ground, the stranger the scene before them seemed. Now that they could see clearly what was happening, they were completely bewildered.

The people on the ground were scrubbing the pavement. That much was clear, but why were they washing the streets? And, what was even more puzzling, why were they doing it without brushes or rags, but with their bare hands?

But Emil and Karl didn't have much time to wonder. The man in the uniform turned them over to someone else. He raised his hand and said, "Jewboys!"

"Very good!" said the other man in a calm, cold voice. And then, without warning, he shouted so loud that Emil and Karl froze. "Don't just stand there! Get down on the ground right now and start washing—and make it fast!"

Emil and Karl dropped to the ground as if they had been shot. Immediately they began to rub the pavement back and forth. The two boys found themselves in a group of several dozen people, in the middle of which was a basin of water. There were four or five uniformed men who stood there, watching them.

"Dip your hands in the bowl! Don't scrub with dry hands!" Emil and Karl dipped their hands into the water and rubbed the stones.

After dipping his hands into the water about a dozen times, Karl's hands began to burn. The skin and even the bones of his hands were inflamed. When he dipped his hands into the bowl it felt as though he was putting them into fire.

Karl examined his hands. They even looked as if they had been set on fire. He stopped scrubbing the stones. He felt that if he rubbed them even one more time, he would scream from the pain, and he didn't want to scream out loud.

Emil wasn't far away, hunched over. Karl watched his friend scrubbing the pavement rapidly with his hands and crying softly to himself.

"Emil, Emil!" Karl called to him, but Emil didn't hear. How could he do it, Karl thought. How could he work with his hands like that, dipping them into that basin of burning water?

Perhaps because he's crying, Karl said to himself. It's better to cry.

Karl's hands hurt so much that he wished he

could get rid of them. If someone were to chop them off, he would feel much better. Even though they were filthy, he could see through the dirt how swollen and red his hands had become. In some places the skin was torn and dark blood was running out of the wounds.

One of the overseers kicked him.

"Get to work! No loafing! Dirty Jew!"

All at once, without knowing why, something flashed through his head—

"Maybe it's because Emil is a Jew?"

Karl didn't understand clearly, but he continued to repeat over and over—

"Maybe because he's a Jew?"

He plunged his hands quickly into the basin and rubbed the pavement.

"Because he's a Jew! Because he's a Jew!"

It became a little easier for him to wash the stones—not much, but a little bit easier. Back and forth he scrubbed to the words "Jew," "Jew," as if he were moving to the ticking of a clock.

Someone blew a blast on a whistle, then another. Everyone stopped working. They raised their heads. A huge man stood over them. Emil and Karl used this opportunity to move closer together. The man spoke, smiling. He spoke gently, pronouncing each word distinctly, as if each one came out of his mouth with a little smile. Neither Emil nor Karl understood very much of what he said, but they were glad to have a chance to rest their hands.

The man continued to speak and to smile. He spoke about the children of Israel, who were being given the opportunity to return to the beginnings of their history. They were replaying it from the very start:

"But there, in ancient Egypt, they made bricks without straw. Now they wash stones without brushes, but with their bare hands. It's almost the same thing."

And the man added, with a little smile, "With their clean, intelligent hands, with their delicate little hands that hate to work.

"But the children of Israel will never escape from this Egypt.

"Oh, no!" said the man, softly but clearly, and again with his little smile, which now made Karl burn, just like the water in the basin.

"In this Egypt the children of Israel will die, die, die!"

There was another whistle blast. Once more everyone crawled, like snakes, and scrubbed the pavement. The men in uniform refilled the empty basins from large bottles. The overseers ran back and forth, stepping on hands and on heads. Some people, who bore the brunt of the overseers' boots more than the others, lay on the ground, motionless.

People were moaning and screaming. Karl screamed with them. It felt good to scream along with everyone else. It seemed to make things easier.

Near Karl was a man dressed in a frock coat and top hat. He scrubbed the stones very rapidly. Three or four overseers stood around him, and each time that the top hat fell off his head they forced him to put it on again right away. When the hat was back on top of his head they laughed wildly.

Then all at once the man stopped and began to shout.

"I can't do any more! I can't do any more! I can't stand this any longer!"

The overseers grabbed him and dragged him off. They took him so far away that he disappeared from sight. The top hat still lay on the ground near Karl.

chapter nine

The overseers continued to herd the hundreds of men and women huddled on the ground. The men in uniform didn't let people stay in any one place for very long but kept them moving. Emil and Karl saw that they should try to stay close together.

Some people were pulled from the sidewalks into the middle of the street. The traffic was heavy. Cars whizzed by quickly, back and forth, and the men in uniform enjoyed watching as the people scrubbing the pavement barely escaped getting run over. They laughed at the sight of men and women scrambling on all fours to save themselves. Some of the drivers started chasing after these terrified people with their cars. They steered their cars this way and that, as if they were just about to run someone over. Usually a driver would pick on one person, and there would be a sort of contest between the driver and his target, who ran every which way to avoid a certain death. This joke caused the overseers to convulse with laughter. They were so amused by it that they began to herd more and more people into the street.

Emil began to feel sick to his stomach. He was very hungry, but if he were given something to eat now, he wouldn't have been able to take a bite. He felt sick from head to toe. Everything began to swim in front of his eyes.

The top hat still lay on the ground near Karl. A man with a long gray beard was now washing the stones near him. He worked very quickly, as though he wanted to get the job over with as fast as possible. As he worked the old man hummed a tune to himself.

Karl could hear the tune clearly; it was both sad and happy. The man with the beard was very small. Down on the ground where they were, it seemed as though he wasn't much bigger than Karl.

All at once some of the men in uniform noticed the old man as well as the top hat that lay on the ground between him and Karl. One of the overseers tore off the cap that the old man was wearing and put the top hat on his head.

The old man looked strange in the top hat, which was far too big for him and kept falling over his eyes. He had to keep pushing it back, but the hat fell down as soon as he started scrubbing the pavement again.

Soon a small circle of about a dozen men in

uniform had gathered around the old man, all shaking with laughter. One of them laughed so hard that he fell down. The old man kept pushing the hat back, but the wide brim kept falling down each time he moved.

All the while, Karl clearly heard that the old man kept humming his little tune. He could even hear the strange words that the old man was singing.

"*Oy, yo, te, ti-di-day, daylom, daylom. Oy, yo, te, ti-di-day, daylom, daylom.*"

The louder the group laughed, the bolder the old man became, and he sang all the louder.

"*Oy, yo, te, ti-di-day, daylom, daylom. Oy, yo, te, ti-di-day, daylom, daylom.*"

Karl couldn't understand why they were laughing so much. The old man was performing a feat that couldn't be easily matched. He scrubbed the stones and adjusted the top hat with such skill that he was a sight to behold. Yet it seemed that the man's very agility was causing the overseers to laugh so hard that they almost collapsed.

Then the group grew tired of this game, and they ran off somewhere else. Karl saw that another group had gathered in a different place to amuse themselves, but he couldn't tell what was going on over there.

Suddenly Emil groaned.

"I'm sick."

"There, there, son," said the old man, cautiously giving him a pat on the head. "You've got to be strong! Where do you feel sick, son?"

"I hurt all over, and I feel sick to my stomach, too," Emil moaned to the old man.

"You mustn't get sick. Better that *they* should be sick, not us.

"If we get sick, then we won't be able to hold out," the old man said, all the while working and fixing the top hat with the same agility, even though no one was standing over him any more.

"I don't feel good," Emil said quietly. He was getting paler and paler.

"Listen, son," the old man said, and he started singing his little song, "Listen to this, and you'll forget that you feel sick."

"*Daylom, daylom, oy, yo, te, ti-di-day, daylom.*"

Emil listened to the song, and it reminded him of his own grandfather's singing. His grandfather had been a tailor. He used to wear a skullcap while he was working. He would spit on his iron, and when the iron sizzled, he'd sing the same way—*daylom, daylom.*

Karl moved closer to the old man. Now he was in the middle, between the two boys.

"That's the way, fellows. Such nice Jewish boys, may God bless you. May God bless you, *daylom*, *daylom*."

He worked with great agility, and the boys worked enthusiastically alongside him.

Suddenly, all three of them noticed an overseer standing there, watching them. Emil and Karl trembled with fear, and they started working even faster. The officer was an older man, and his face was wrinkled and sallow. He bent over and asked the old man, "How long have the children been working?"

Emil and Karl heard the way that he called them "children"; it almost seemed to be kind.

This encouraged Karl, and he answered, "For a long time, since breakfast."

"You can go home. That will be enough for you."

Emil was about to say that he didn't have a home, but he stopped. He was afraid it would lead to more questions, and he wanted to get away as quickly as possible.

"Can we go?" Karl asked again, because he couldn't believe this sudden turn of luck.

"Yes, children, you can go." And then he added, "As a matter of fact, I'll lead you away from here, until you're out of danger."

Emil was the first to get up and the first to let out

a moan. It felt as though he'd been broken into several pieces. He couldn't stand up straight.

"Whoever brought you here is—" the overseer's face grew red as fire. Several times he opened his mouth to say something, but he stopped. "Whoever brought you here is a great big fool. Come!"

He carefully helped Karl up from the ground. Karl also could barely stand up straight. The man accidentally touched the boy's hand. Karl flinched in pain and waved his hand back and forth, as though he'd just been scalded.

"Are you in much pain?" the overseer asked, drily.

Karl bit his lip. Tears ran from his eyes, and his heart was heavy.

"Yes! It hurts something awful."

The overseer had already started to walk away, but he turned around and said to the old man, "That's enough for you, too, old man. You've already done your share."

The old man held the top hat with one hand and asked with a calm face, "Me? Why me? What did I do to deserve this? Thank God, I still have the strength to stay here with my brothers. Wait, you'll see, because you are rescuing these children, God will reward you."

"Get up!" said the man in uniform, almost

shouting. He picked up the old man's cap, which lay nearby, and handed it to him. He pulled the top hat off the old man's head, threw it on the ground, and stamped on it.

"Get up, get up!" he ordered, "And come with me."

The old man rose slowly. First he smoothed out his beard, as though that was the only part of him that had gotten rumpled while he was crouching on the ground. When he stood up straight, he looked sharply at the overseer. He was perhaps half the size of the man in uniform, but he looked at him fearlessly.

"What will become of all of the others? Who will help them?" he said, almost angrily. "Won't they still be here, crawling around, even after I've escaped?"

The overseer didn't reply. The creases in his face became even heavier, like a sheet of rumpled paper.

"Old man, you're asking me about things I can't explain. You'd better go away from here."

The old man became a little calmer. Emil and Karl huddled next to him.

"Well, of course," he said. "A man can't just explain it away."

"Yes, you're right, a man can't explain it away—

certainly not just one man. Each one of us is powerless by himself."

Several young men in uniform passed by. They all saluted the overseer with great respect. He responded with a raised hand and a stern face.

The old man stood there, taking a last look at the great mass of men and women huddled on the square. He closed his eyes and mumbled something.

They reached another street, where everything seemed calm and quiet—much calmer and quieter than usual. The overseer stopped.

"Very well, you can now be quite sure that no one will bother you any more," and he started to walk away.

But Karl stopped him, tugging at the man's sleeve.

"I want to ask you something. I just want to ask you a simple question."

"Go ahead, don't be afraid!" the man said. "Ask me whatever you like."

Karl thought, trying to put the words together inside his head, but all at once he blurted out, "What makes them do it?" He looked at the overseer with large, blue, inquiring eyes.

The man in uniform stood silently for several minutes and looked at the children. He didn't say a single word, and walked away. Emil and Karl turned around several times to see if he was looking back at them—but no, he walked away quickly, until he was out of sight.

The old man practically danced for joy.

"My, you are a clever fellow, you certainly asked him the right question. 'What makes them do it?' That's just the thing to ask."

The man was so happy that he began to sing his little song again.

"Oy, daylom, daylom, ya-te, ti-di-day, daylom, day-lom."

Suddenly he stopped and smacked his forehead with his hand.

"I forgot it already! How could I forget such a wonderful question! You must repeat it for me at least once, what was it that you asked him?"

Karl began to sense that there was a strange purpose to his own question. He repeated it twice.

"What makes them do it? What makes them do it?"

"It's as precious as gold! You really asked him the right question. He'll never forget it. You saw how he walked away without saying a thing, didn't you? No, he's never going to forget it. You can't forget a question like that so easily."

chapter ten

The old man walked on. Emil and Karl trudged after him, heading in no particular direction, down streets that didn't seem to lead anywhere. The boys had no idea where they were going and they didn't care.

Emil was no longer scared. What had happened to him that day was worse, much worse, than anything he had ever feared. He walked with indifferent steps; it didn't matter to him in the least where they led.

Emil felt that now he was quite grown up. He even decided he would not cry any more. He looked at his reflection in a window as they walked along and was surprised to see that he hadn't grown any taller. It was reassuring, though, when he noticed that the old man was also short, not much taller than Emil himself.

The old man couldn't stop marveling at them.

"You're such wonderful boys, may God watch over you! You're going to make your parents very happy. May you only have God's help, may He only have mercy on us."

"We don't have any parents," Karl said.

The old man stopped and stood still.

"No mother and no father?"

"No," Karl answered.

"Not you and not him?" the old man asked in a frightened voice.

"Our fathers are dead, and our mothers are gone, too."

"Orphans—poor things, no parents at all," the old man said, as if to himself.

Emil wanted to tell him what had happened to his parents and to Karl's parents, but he felt that it would be too much to explain. And now it didn't matter to him, nothing did. He didn't feel like saying a single word.

Karl was the first to cry out when he recognized the street.

"Look, Emil, we're not far from your home. And from there it's only two steps to mine."

"Whom do you live with, boys?" asked the old man.

Karl felt somewhat embarrassed about getting so excited and shouting "your" home and "mine." He lowered his head.

"We used to live here," he said, adding, "but now we're staying with some friends. The janitor of the building where I used to live took us in. He's a good man, and his wife is, too."

"Thank God. Thank God," the old man said. "Well, of course—after all, are there no decent people left at all? There are still some good ones here on earth. They're still here," he said, and his face glowed with happiness.

"So, I bid you farewell. May God watch over you," the old man said.

"Good-bye, Zeyde," said Emil.

"You're a fine young man," said the old man, happily, giving his cheek a pinch.

As the old man walked away, Karl wondered what the word "Zeyde" meant. Emil explained that it's what they used to call his grandfather.

Karl didn't want to be thought any less of than Emil, and he ran after the old man.

"Good-bye, Zeyde," he said, panting. "You're a Zeyde, you're my Zeyde, too."

A smile spread over the old man's entire face. He stroked his beard and started to say something, but he couldn't. He patted Karl's head, and then he began to sing the little melody that he'd sung as they were scrubbing the pavement.

Karl suddenly felt so happy! Now that he heard

the melody one more time, he was sure that he'd never forget it.

"Your song is very beautiful," Karl said, delighted.

"What, do you think it's just mine?" said the old man. "Believe me, this melody is even older than I am. My father used to sing it, and his father did, too."

"It's a Zeyde-song," said Karl.

"That's it, you've got it. Now, do you know what I wish for you? I hope that you will grow up and, someday, you'll be a Zeyde yourself."

When Karl returned to Emil, he found his friend standing in the same place, lost in thought.

"I like him," said Karl.

"Me too," said Emil.

"We're never going to forget him," said Karl.

"But we don't even know his name," Emil observed.

"Didn't you say that his name is Zeyde?" Karl wondered out loud. "That's really easy to remember."

They walked toward the building where Karl lived. Everything there was still. All the windows were shut. The only living creature they saw was a kitten warming itself in the sun and yawning.

"You see," said Karl, "there's the kitten from the cellar. It's waiting for us."

They walked down the few steps to the cellar and opened the door.

The janitor's wife jumped up.

"Where have you been, children? I didn't know what to think. You've been gone for over five hours."

Emil was surprised to hear her say "over five hours." To him it seemed as though five weeks had passed since he and Karl had wandered away from the house. And what hadn't happened to them in those five hours!

Karl started to explain, but suddenly he saw that Berta's eyes were full of tears.

"Where is Josef?" he asked, frightened, looking around the dark basement room.

The janitor's wife suddenly burst out crying. She sobbed and sobbed, unable to control herself.

When she began to calm down, she told them that a few hours earlier storm troopers had come and arrested him. They'd also arrested Herr Schneidmesser, who lived upstairs.

"Herr Schneidmesser is the man who gave us the meat," Karl said softly to Emil.

Karl didn't know what came over him. He wanted to kick someone, to scream at someone, but he didn't know whom. Who was doing all of these things? He looked up at the ceiling, and it seemed to him as if the entire building would collapse any minute. The place was full of holes. His own apartment was empty, the Gutenglass's apartment was empty, Herr Schneidmesser was arrested, Josef was arrested. There was no way that building would be able to withstand it. It would have to fall down.

The janitor's wife washed both boys' hands gently with warm water. She looked at their red, swollen hands and cried once more.

Emil's pants were torn at both knees; Karl's were torn only at the right knee. She undressed them both and put warm compresses on their wounds.

She gave them hot soup to eat. Emil ate without much appetite, but Karl ate heartily, and he continued to talk about washing the pavement, the overseer who saved them, and Zeyde.

Later she put the two boys to bed and mended their torn trousers.

"It's still early," Berta said, "but you must be very tired. Just lie in bed if you can't fall asleep."

It felt so good to be in bed. The warmth helped soothe their aching bones.

"My feet and hands hurt," Karl complained.

"I hurt all over," Emil responded, "My head, too."

The janitor's wife quietly sewed patches onto

their pants and listened as Karl talked and talked. From time to time she asked a question without raising her head from her work.

"What did the overseer who saved you look like?" she asked.

"Oh, he was older than the others, and his face was hard, it looked so serious. I would recognize him if I saw him on the street," Karl said.

"Me too," Emil added.

"And I would definitely recognize Zeyde," Karl said, "But not the others. They all looked the same, they all had the same uniform and the same face."

"That's very true, only good people have a face. You can recognize good people, but bad people all look the same," she said quite softly, as if to herself.

Karl thought about what she said, and Emil was quiet, too.

"It's strange, but that's really the way it is," said Karl, recalling how all the good people he'd met had looked. He even remembered the rabbi who had been in Emil's home. But he couldn't recall the faces of the three men who had taken away his mother.

When Berta had finished with their trousers she put out the lights.

"It's late," she said in the darkness. "Tomorrow will be sunny, and we'll figure out what to do with you. I have to go to my mother's; there's nothing for me to do here. I'm all alone here, and my mother lives far away. It takes four, five hours by train. But I won't abandon you, you can be sure of that. Good night, children."

Karl began to feel very sad. He was worried about what the next day's plans might be.

"Good night," he answered.

He listened and wondered why Emil didn't say anything. But then he heard him breathing heavily, like someone fast asleep.

"Emil's sleeping," Karl said, explaining why his friend hadn't said good night.

"Poor little boy," Bertha said. "He's completely worn out."

chapter eleven

In the morning Karl awoke to discover a pair of brown, smiling eyes, and for a brief moment he thought he was looking at his mother. Still half asleep, he enjoyed the warmth of her smile.

But as he emerged from sleep, he realized that it was the sad smile of the janitor's wife. She stood bent over a small suitcase and kept pushing down on it with her knee to get more clothes to fit inside.

Emil was already sitting in a chair, drinking a glass of milk. He looked refreshed, his shirt had been washed and pressed, and he had been scrubbed completely clean.

Karl saw that it was sunny outside. Some pale light seeped in through the cellar window, and the room was pleasantly quiet.

"We've been waiting for you long enough," Emil greeted him.

Only then did Karl wake up completely. Until he heard Emil's voice, his eyes kept opening and closing.

Karl jumped out of bed and was about to grab his shirt, which was waiting for him, washed and pressed, on a chair next to the bed.

"Oh, no," said the janitor's wife. "That won't do. First you have to give yourself a good washing."

She gave him a basin of cold water, and he started to splash about, almost as if he were going for a swim. He liked cold water and would always splash some on his face whenever he wanted to wake himself up.

But the janitor's wife didn't let him fool around for long. She took him in her hands and washed and scrubbed him. She rubbed him with soap until it felt as though she was scrubbing beneath his skin. Then she combed his hair, parting it in the middle.

Now Emil and Karl looked at one another happily. Emil remembered when they used to meet in the schoolyard. That was a happy time, when all the children would still play with him.

As he recalled those days, Emil's heart felt heavy. He began to think about what had happened since then, and he couldn't believe it. He tried to remember how long it had been since that night when his father had been beaten and dragged from the house. He started to count—a night, a day, a day, a night—but he got confused.

He could only remember that when he had left

his house he was all alone in the world. He had no one except for his friend Karl. Emil suddenly realized how grateful he felt to Berta, who was now making breakfast. He went over and embraced her.

She didn't move away, but shut her eyes and put her arms around him as tears ran down her face.

"Come here, Karl, come to me," Berta called out and embraced both boys. "Things will get better, they will. Today we'll say good-bye to each other, but Josef will come back, and we'll be happy again."

Still, tears still continued to run down her face.

Emil felt much freer and happier. Later, as he and Karl walked with Berta to the park, he felt much more at ease than the day before, when he had run, terrified, out of the house.

But as soon as they reached the park they heard wild cries and laughter. Emil almost broke away from Bertha's grasp. She wanted to run herself but froze with fear, holding both children firmly by the hand.

The park was small, and Emil and Karl knew every corner of it. They often took walks there on Sundays. Now it was packed with people standing about. Even if Emil and Karl had wanted to run away, there was no way that they could have pushed their way through the crowd. People kept running through the gate toward them, and there was simply no place to move.

The shrieks and laughter sent chills through them. A storm trooper in uniform ran ahead of them and stopped Berta.

"Are you an Aryan?" he asked.

She nodded her head.

He took a hard look at her and at the two children. Then he smiled.

"Very well, ma'am, go on in with your children. They'll find it very amusing."

Numb with fear, Berta walked into the thick of the crowd and pulled the two children after her.

She forced her way through to an open spot. A few people shouted and complained that she was pushing them.

"How rude! Why all this shoving?"

Berta felt like turning back, but other people stuck up for her.

"Let the children be entertained. Aryan children need to be amused," they said, looking affectionately at the boys, their faces glowing happily.

Once more Berta approached an open spot. Other mothers and fathers with their children pushed forward along with her.

There was a large circle in the middle of the park. Dozens of men, women, and children stood inside the circle. Karl noticed right away that they were different from the rest of this Sunday crowd.

"Look—they're Jews!" Emil cried out.

Berta put her hand over his mouth. Emil wanted to shout again, but her warm hand restrained him.

Dozens of storm troopers also stood in the circle. Near Emil and Karl a man staggered about, barely able to stay on his feet. He began clapping his hands and whistling.

"C'mon, let's get started! The German people are impatient!"

Many others started clapping, too.

"They've been dragging these damned Jews out of their houses all morning. They pulled all of them out of our building," said a young woman with a parasol, smiling.

"Careful with that umbrella! You'll poke someone's eye out," people warned her.

"They cleaned all the Jews out of our place, too," a tall thin man, who looked as though he were standing on stilts, said in a loud voice.

"What's going to happen now?" asked a man who had only just elbowed his way through the crowd.

"He has no idea what's going on," someone else said, making fun of him. "These lousy Jews are going to amuse us Aryans."

"Terrific!" the man shouted. "We deserve no less. They ought to make it a law to do this every Sunday."

"Yes, they really should make it a law. Only it's a pity that the storm troopers have to work so hard! They've been dragging Jews here since dawn."

The man who'd started the clapping began to clap even louder. It could be heard everywhere.

"C'mon, let's start! We're suffocating from this heat!"

Mothers kept pushing forward with their children.

"Stop shoving! How rude! It's so crowded, we'll suffocate!"

"Let the children move up! It's their treat," other people suggested.

"No!" protests came from all sides. "This is for everyone. Grown-ups should be entertained, too!"

"That's right," dozens of others agreed. "Everyone wants to see."

"Why are you pushing?" people said to the lady, who by now had closed her parasol.

"I want to see my Jews, the ones from my building, I want to see them when it's their turn. That would be wonderful."

"We all want to see! We all want to see our Jews!" dozens of people shouted from among the crowd.

The man began clapping even louder. Then, suddenly, little pieces of red and green paper rained down on the crowd. All around, people looked up to see where this colorful shower came from.

Thousands of pieces of paper fell on the crowd. Many got caught in the trees or stuck to people's hats. Karl picked up a red piece. There was something printed on it, in fat, black letters:

FOR SHAME! DON'T LET THE AUSTRIAN PEOPLE BECOME ANIMALS!

chapter twelve

All at once, dozens of storm troopers rushed through the crowd. Emil and Karl were shoved aside and were almost torn away from Berta. There was a great deal of shouting and confusion. People in the crowd were screaming.

Suddenly everyone ran off to one corner of the park. Emil and Karl were swept along with them.

Two storm troopers there were beating a man. The man's face was no longer recognizable. It was completely swollen, and blood ran from his eyes, his ears, his nose. It seemed as though he was weeping blood.

"I am one-hundred-percent Aryan," he pleaded in a weak voice. "You'll pay dearly for this! You'll pay for this!"

The storm troopers continued to strike him.

"Where'd you get that red piece of paper?" One of the men in uniform asked.

"I picked it up off the ground. I'm an Aryan!"

He collapsed, and the storm troopers left him lying on the ground.

Screams came from the other side of the park. The entire crowd ran over.

"That's him!" some shouted. "He's the one who scattered those papers!"

One old woman yelled louder than the rest: "I saw him tossing them into the air. I saw it myself!"

But before the storm troopers could reach him, the man pulled some documents out from his shirt pocket.

"Here are my papers," he shouted in a loud voice, trying to be heard over the crowd.

The soldiers examined his papers carefully, and then they raised their hands, saluting him.

"*Heil!*" he answered.

The people in the crowd all raised their hands as well.

"They could kill an innocent person," someone muttered.

"Yes. And whoever scattered those papers was very clever about it."

"What does it say on them?" a short man asked.

"Pick one up and take a look. Why don't you pick one up?" another man answered with a taunting laugh.

The first man just stood there, not knowing what to do, and looked down at the trampled pieces of paper.

People began to run back to the spot where they had all crowded together before.

"Let's go home," Emil quietly said to Berta.

But she didn't reply. In all the commotion, Berta didn't even hear that Emil had said something to her.

"Please, you'll step on the children!" she said to the people around them.

"The children! The children!" they shouted with her.

Emil and Karl could no longer find a place to stand. They made their way to one corner of the park, but they could still see dozens of men, women, and children standing in a circle, surrounded by storm troopers.

A big, broad-shouldered man with a wild red beard and a head of scruffy red hair stood taller than the rest of the crowd. He wore an old jacket, its color faded beyond recognition, and tight-fitting shorts that just reached the top of his knees.

He let out a laugh that rolled like a barrel and ended in a shriek. Each time he laughed he clapped his hands together and yelled, "This is good! This is good!"

Then he stretched out his hand and gave a wild shout: "*Heil! Heil!*"

His face swelled and grew stern. His cheeks were so puffed up that it looked as though they were about to burst.

But just when it seemed that his eyes would pop out of his head from shouting "*Heil,*" he burst into a peal of laughter that ended in a shriek.

"This is good! This is good!" he said, his feet dancing.

"Idiot! Be quiet!"

"*Heil!*" he shouted with all his might. Then, like an army called into action, the crowd began to raise their hands and shouted back, "*Heil!*"

After this chorus of *Heil*'s he burst out laughing once more. His laughter was infectious. A few children started imitating the peculiar way that he laughed, and the whole crowd was delighted. Emil and Karl moved closer to him, and for a moment they forgot where they were. From the circle in the middle of the park, they could hear a man in uniform speaking, but he was too far away for the boys to understand what he was saying. The red-haired man was laughing so loudly, and the crowd along with him, that it was impossible to hear a word.

Suddenly they saw a soldier pick out one of the

people from the group in the circle and lead him over to a tree.

The man scurried up the tree just like a squirrel. He climbed up to the very top and stayed there, sitting among the branches.

The whole crowd lunged forward, breaking through the dozens of storm troopers who were trying to keep them from getting too close.

Now they could hear everything. The soldier standing under the tree ordered the man above him to make sounds like a bird.

No response came from the tree.

"Crow like a rooster," the soldier shouted.

From the tree a weak "cock-a-doodle-doo" could be heard.

"Louder!" The officer yelled.

The man up in the branches crowed louder now. The crowd went wild and applauded, as if they were watching a play. The red-haired man danced about, clapping his hands and shouting loudly, "This is good! This is good!"

When the man in the tree came down, the soldier hit him on the head twice. A second man was already waiting to take his place. He was an old man. He tried to climb the tree, but he couldn't make his way up. Each time he fell down, the storm trooper struck him, and the entire crowd shook with laughter.

But there was no way that he could get up the tree. After he'd been hit several times, he could no longer stay on his feet, so the officers forced him to sing as he lay on the ground.

The old man sang in such a peculiar voice that the storm troopers went berserk.

"Louder!" they shouted. "Even louder!"

But the more the officers shouted, the softer the old man's voice became.

Then it seemed that everything went crazy, like an insane asylum. Under the storm troopers' orders the people in the circle started to sing in a strange mix of voices. Their children wailed along with them. Dozens of people crawled on the ground, chewing on the grass and calling out "moo!" or barking "bow-wow!" Others were ordered to sit in the trees, crowing and trilling like birds.

And above all this tumult the red-haired man's "*Heil! Heil!*" and his raucous laughter could still be heard.

"This is good! This is good!"

Suddenly a shot rang out. The crowd shuddered and started to run away. The gunshot came from within the circle. Karl had seen it—a finely dressed man with silver-gray hair had pointed the revolver at himself. Now he fell, the revolver still in his hand.

People began to push closer, right up to the spot where the man with the revolver lay. Several storm troopers ran past and kicked him in the stomach. The revolver fell out of his hand.

One of the soldiers bent over, raised the man's bloody head, and spoke to the onlookers, as if he were reciting a poem:

"How beautifully they die, these children of Israel! How excellent!"

The crowd began to disperse. Many people began to make their way out of the park, heading down the side streets. Others were so exhausted that they dropped onto the grass, as if they had fainted.

Berta took advantage of this opportunity and headed for the gate with Emil and Karl.

But then she, too, sat down for a while on the grass.

"I have to rest. I can't move my feet."

Emil wanted to say something, but Berta interrupted him.

"Don't talk now, Emil, not one word!"

"Yes," Karl added, "Don't say anything."

Another woman came over and sat down near Berta. She was stooped, like an old woman, though her face didn't look old at all. She sat hunched over, as though she felt cold on such a hot, humid day.

"What a day this has been!" she mumbled, as if to herself. Then she turned to Berta. "How did you like it? Nice?"

Berta started to move away from her.

The woman snapped at her. "You don't have to run away from me. I'm not going to bite you. How do you like our Vienna?" she asked again.

"I don't know, I'm just a janitor's wife, an ignorant woman!" she blurted.

"I'm just an ignorant woman, too," the stranger said.

The women looked at each other without saying anything for a while.

"Nice boys," the woman said. "Handsome boys."

"Come," Berta said to Emil and Karl. "Time to go."

But as soon as she started to get up, the woman grabbed her by the hand.

"You don't have to run away from me, I'm your friend."

She spoke quietly, but so gently and kindly that Berta stayed where she was, and so did Emil and Karl.

Berta summoned all her courage and asked,

"How do you know that we're friends?"

"That's easy—when I spoke to you, you said nothing. Silence says a great deal."

The stranger stroked Karl's hair and at the same time caressed Emil.

"In that case, I'd like to ask your advice. My husband's gone. These boys aren't mine; their situation is very bad. Today I have to leave the city. Someone has to look after these boys. Someone!" the janitor's wife said quickly.

"Your husband's gone?" The woman bent over even closer and added softly, "Was he arrested?"

Berta didn't answer. Her teary eyes spoke for her.

"You can turn the boys over to me. I'll make sure that no harm comes to them," the woman said.

"Their situation is very bad. They have no mothers, they have no fathers, they have no roof over their heads. They need to be taken care of."

The stranger answered in a dry but insistent voice. "You can trust them to me."

"Emil, Karl, do you want to go with this woman? I have to go away. If I stay in the city I'll have no way of getting food, I have to go to my mother."

The two boys went over to the woman and looked her in the eye.

Karl was the first to answer that he was ready to

go with her. Emil nodded his head in agreement.

Emil took hold of Berta and kissed her hand.

"No farewells," the stranger insisted. Turning to the janitor's wife, she said, "Go, and don't look back."

Berta remained seated.

"I feel like a criminal for leaving the children, but I have no choice."

"You don't have to worry about them at all. Just pick yourself up and go."

They heard a group of laughing men and women approach. A storm trooper walked along with them, his laughter ringing out above the rest.

"Go!" the stranger shouted.

Berta rose and walked out the main gate.

"We can go now, too."

The stranger and the boys got up as well, and they set out through a different entrance to the park.

chapter thirteen

Emil and Karl walked in silence. The stranger kept them moving at a quick pace.

"You'll see, boys, you'll be quite fine with me. You won't have to worry about a thing."

Karl looked up at her and smiled, but Emil looked at her with eyes full of tears.

"My name is Matilda. You can call me Aunt Matilda. I'm a good cook, and I'll make you the nicest meals. In fact, we can already start thinking about lunch. What should we have as soon as we get home? You must be very hungry."

"No," the boys answered, "We aren't hungry at all."

"Not even a bit? Let's close our eyes and think about a warm bowl of soup, some roast veal, a piece of fruit, and a nice slice of cake."

Karl started to laugh, and Emil smiled weakly.

"That's what Aunt Matilda likes. She loves happy children. In your new home you'll be able to play as much as your heart desires."

Suddenly Karl asked in a serious voice, "Will we go to school, too?"

"No-o," Aunt Matilda answered slowly. "No going to school. But I'll study with you every day, and you'll learn much better than you would in school."

Karl felt a little happier. He even began to swing Matilda's hand back and forth as they walked along, faster than before.

"Emil, don't slow down," Karl called out. "Let's keep the same pace."

Emil, who also held Aunt Matilda by the hand, started imitating his friend. Now the two boys were leading Matilda, and she skipped along between them.

But all at once Emil became distracted. He slowed down, and Aunt Matilda noticed it right away.

"Emil," she said, rousing him, "if you're going to daydream instead of keeping up with us, then we'll all fall down. We're all linked together."

Emil got back in step with them. Aunt Matilda laughed, and the boys began to sing a song that they'd learned in school.

Then Karl noticed that they were no longer on paved streets. They were now walking on sand that was black with coal dust. The path was dusty. Karl walked more slowly, because with each step he kicked up a lot of dust that tickled his nose and throat.

In the distance they heard chugging and whistling. A train with many cars rode by through the tall, dry grass, leaving a thick cloud of black smoke. Karl started counting. But the train moved too fast for him, and he wasn't sure if it had sixteen or eighteen cars. By this time Emil had let go of Aunt Matilda's hand as well. He stood, staring at the train, full of curiosity and fear.

Karl wanted to say something to Emil. A story had started to take shape inside his head. This Aunt Matilda was leading them astray, taking them into the woods somewhere. There they'd be sold to bandits, who would force them to be criminals, too. Later, when they were grown up, they would steal enough money to buy their freedom.

But even Karl didn't find this story frightening. Aunt Matilda looked at both boys with a smile. She pointed at the tall grass. "The tracks run through the grass, and the train moves on its very own steel path. Now we're outside the city. Do you see that hut? That's where the signalman lives. A lot of trains stop there, and he waves them on with a little flag. See, not far from his hut"—she pointed to a small, dark house that stood a few dozen steps from the hut— "that's where we live. We'll be home very soon."

The sand became deeper. Small, sharp pebbles got into their shoes, and the walk grew harder and harder. The smoke from the train began to disperse, leaving behind a heavy smell.

Aunt Matilda led them onto a smooth path. From there they could see the train tracks, which lay like long, sharp swords that sparkled in the sun.

"Before you cross the tracks you have to look carefully in both directions. Do you know why?" Matilda asked them.

"Because a train might be coming," they both answered together.

"Yes, you have to be very careful, because a train can come by without warning."

And just as they were standing there, they again heard a loud chugging. This time a train with an end-less number of cars crawled slowly past. Hundreds of chickens and ducks looked out from some of the cars. The chickens blinked at them without making a sound, but the ducks made so much noise that they could be heard for miles. Emil and Karl laughed out loud. Even the sorry-looking chickens made them laugh. In the last few cars there were some horses. They held their heads stiffly, their eyes showing no sign of curiosity—they didn't even look around to see where they were. Only one young pony neighed, as if it were sneezing because something got into its nostrils.

"It's a freight train. That's why it's moving so slowly," Matilda said. "Only passenger trains go fast; chickens and ducks and horses travel slowly."

In front of the signal hut stood an old man with a cap pulled down over his eyes. He waved a flag up and down. People stuck their heads out from a few of the cars. They looked just as bored as the horses. They exchanged a few idle words with the signalman as the train moved slowly by. One of them laughed, but his laughter was dry and smoky, like the thick, heavy smoke from the locomotive.

Emil and Karl followed Aunt Matilda with tired footsteps and looked longingly at the freight train and its dingy cars.

The path to the second house went uphill a bit. From there the freight train looked like a contorted giant, doubled over with a stomachache.

Aunt Matilda knocked on the door several times. When it opened, Karl froze in place, unable to move. Emil gasped, his throat tightening with fear and surprise.

There in the doorway stood the very same man, the one with the scruffy red hair and the curly beard, who'd been in the crowd at the park laughing and shouting *Heil*. He no longer had on his jacket, but he was still wearing the same tight, short pants that came to the top of his knees.

When he saw Emil and Karl, he blinked his watery blue eyes. But straight away he puffed up his cheeks and yelled, *"Heil! Heil!"*

Emil was so terrified that he almost raised his hand in salute, but it wouldn't budge. Karl held on to Aunt Matilda.

The red-haired man burst into his coarse laugh that ended in a shriek, but this time it lasted longer and sounded pleasant, like the laughter of a child.

"He's harmless. He doesn't bother anyone. He won't do you any harm. He loves children very much. He's a child himself, a grown-up child."

The red-haired man puffed up his cheeks and popped them with his fists, as if they were balloons. He danced and sang and shouted, "This is good! This is good!"

The children began to get used to him, but each time that he puffed up his cheeks, squinted his eyes, and shouted *"Heil,"* they became sad. The *Heil* reminded Karl of the brown uniforms of the storm troopers. Emil became completely confused and didn't know what to do. Meanwhile, Matilda began to set the table in the main room of the house. On the right was a narrow little room, and off to the left was another small room that had no windows and was completely dark.

The red-haired man lifted Karl all the way up to the ceiling, and as he held him up, he asked, "Name?"

"Karl," Karl answered.

He took hold of Emil and lifted him up as well.

Emil didn't wait for the question and said his name right away.

The red-haired man sat down and started repeating their names over and over again. When he said "Karl" he pointed his finger at Karl, and pointed at Emil when he said his name. Somewhere along the way he got mixed up and called Karl "Emil." This made the boys laugh, and they taught him their names again. The red-haired man's face grew serious, and he followed their instructions.

When at last he had repeated their names four or five times without making a mistake, he was so excited that he started dancing again and shouted, "This is good, this is good!" Then, in a blink of an eye the tall, heavy man stood on his head and began to kick with his feet, as if he were about to fall over, but he made a quick somersault and stood up.

Karl laughed loudly and tried to imitate him. Emil stood nearby, watching happily.

Aunt Matilda laughed along with them.

"Didn't I tell you that you'd have a good time?"

At the table the red-haired man started to get their names mixed up again. He pronounced Karl's name "Sharl," and he kept calling Emil "Shlemil." Suddenly, as he was eating, his mouth full of food, he banged on the table so hard that the plates rattled.

"My name! My name," he shouted, "is Hans! Hans!"

"Uncle Hans!" Emil and Karl sang out.

"Uncle! Uncle!" The red-haired man danced with glee. "Uncle!"

It made him so happy to hear the boys call him Uncle that he flipped over and stood on his head again. Standing on his head, he let out a whistle like a locomotive. Emil and Karl really thought that a train had just passed by the house.

chapter fourteen

In the evening a man smoking a pipe dropped by. He filled the room with great clouds of smoke even before he took the pipe out of his mouth and said "good evening." He sat in a rocking chair and puffed away.

Matilda was cleaning the house and barely looked at the visitor. Quietly she explained to the children that he was their neighbor, the signalman, who lived in the little hut by the train tracks and who waved to the passing trains with his little flag.

Emil and Karl were curious about the signalman. They moved closer, but when they got near him they smelled a very sharp, unpleasant odor. The signalman's large cap fell down over his eyes. He clenched the stem of his pipe between his teeth and dozed for a bit. Then he awoke with a start and began puffing away on his pipe, trying to get its fire going again.

Hans opened the door, sat down on the threshold, and looked out. A few flies buzzed around the kerosene lamp that stood on the table where they had just finished eating. From time to time Hans let out one of his laughs. Emil sat down next to him and looked out into the dark. He thought about how much he would like to ride on a train.

The signalman woke up once more and puffed on his pipe, but this time he couldn't bring its fire back to life. Slowly he felt each of his pockets, poking and rummaging about, until he pulled out a match. He struck it against the rocking chair. The match lit and immediately went out. Disappointed, the signalman started to suck on the stem of his pipe.

Suddenly he opened his eyes wide and asked, "Who are these boys?"

"Just boys," Matilda answered. "They're good boys."

"Ah!" the signalman responded, as if that was enough information for him.

"Their names are Emil and Karl. This is Emil, and the other boy is Karl," Matilda said, pointing.

"Really?" the signalman said, surprised. "That's very nice."

"And you've been guzzling a bit too much," Matilda said. "Someday you won't even be able to hold that flag in your hand."

"No, today I've barely even wet my lips."

"Is that so!" Matilda said. "You can smell it a mile away."

"Well, what's true is true. Yesterday I did go drinking. My friends took me out and said, 'Have a drink.' The fact is, I have a strong character, but when they put a bottle on the table and say, 'Have a drink'—"

Karl's whole body shivered, and he went to sit in a chair.

"Hans, close the door," Matilda said. "Karl is cold."

"No, I'm not cold," he said, but as he spoke, another shiver ran through him.

"The nights are a little chilly," the signalman said. "Here it's much cooler than in the city. People come here to cool off."

Hans shut the door and started shouting "*Heil.*" The signalman raised his hand lazily with each *Heil*. Emil sat at the table and counted the flies buzzing around the lamp.

The signalman found a match and quickly relit his pipe.

"If I were the same age as these two," he said, pointing to the boys, "I would be grateful to be alive. Which is not to say that things are all that bad nowadays.

"Now, you take Saturday," he continued. "That wasn't so bad. You could even say it was good. After we finished drinking, they said to me, 'Come, Friedrich.' We walked and we walked, until we came to a clothing store. 'Let's go in,' they said, 'and take something without paying for it.' So I said, 'They'll arrest us, just like dogs.' But they laughed, and they said, 'You're an old fool. Don't you know that you can take whatever you want from the Jews, and that they can't say a thing about it? You can even pay them with a slap instead of with money, and they can't say anything.'"

The red-haired man burst out laughing and ended with a *Heil*. The signalman lazily raised his hand in salute.

"And that's just the way it was. Can you believe it? I couldn't believe it, either. But just go take a look in my closet: a brand-new suit, hanging there just like a dead man, and two pairs of shoes—and I took a watch, too. All on Saturday. At one place we also took some money. The people there were so scared, they just gave us everything. Then we went drinking some more."

He took a few puffs on his pipe and rocked back and forth in the chair.

"Now, you can't say that this is all on the level. You could even say it's against the law. And that suit's hanging there, like a dead man. I have strong character, but when someone says to you, 'Take it,' and they give it to you—they give it to you, I swear to God, you go in and they give it to you."

He dozed off for a few minutes, and Hans let out a few of his laughs.

Then the signalman took a watch out of his pocket.

"There's still a good hour until the nine o'clock comes through. Here, take a look at this piece of goods. There are watches, and then there are *watches*. This one is like a sundial. The watchmaker just gave it to me. I swear to God. On the other hand, the Jews are rich. You take a suit from them, they still have three more."

The signalman held out the watch to let all of them take a look at it, but no one took it from him.

"Or course, it is against the law. But somebody says, 'Have a drink'—also, now the laws are all different. I swear to God, I didn't hit anyone. One of us—what's true is true—he beat up this Jewish tailor, and another fellow helped him. Now that's too much, isn't that right, Matilda? There's no need to do any hitting. They'll only bring it all back against you.

"Now I'm a rich man. I have a new suit hanging like a dead man in my closet. Two pairs of shoes—

one pair yellow, one pair black—a watch, and a little bit of pocket money. Still, if I were as young as those two"—he pointed at the boys again—"it would be better, though things aren't bad nowadays. Only you just can't let things get out of hand."

Emil sat with his head lowered. Aunt Matilda sat down next to him and caressed him. She whispered into his ear, "He's an old drunk. Don't let any of his babbling bother you!"

"I hate it when people hit," the signalman said, as he continued to smoke. "My friends don't have any God or any conscience in their hearts any more. They get more pleasure from hitting than from taking things. I don't go for taking things. But if they give it to you, that's different—it's hard to resist. One of our group beat up the watchmaker, he even hit his wife and children. And the watchmaker begged him not to hurt his wife and children."

Hans broke into his hearty laugh, ending with a whining shriek. Then suddenly he began to choke. He coughed and coughed as if trying to force something out of his throat. He twisted around in all directions, as though he were trying to hide his head. Then all at once they all heard that Hans had stopped laughing. He was crying.

The house broke into an uproar. Matilda and

Emil leaped up from the floor. Karl got up from his chair and stood, terrified.

"Calm down, Hans," Matilda said sternly. "Calm down."

Hans began to weep out loud. He buried his head in his hands and sobbed loudly.

"Idiot, why are you crying?" said Friedrich. "You don't have to take it so seriously. If you take a suit from a Jew, he's got three, maybe four more. Of course, hitting goes against your conscience, but I can tell you even worse stories."

Gradually Hans came back to his senses. He saluted several times, shouting *"Heil!"*

"Now you're talking sense," Friedrich said, raising his hand. "What made you start bawling like that? Once an idiot, always an idiot. I tell him about Jews and he cries. But what's true is true—they gave everything away. You walk in the door and they say, 'Take it.' Usually I'm a man of character. But if they say, 'Have a drink,' I drink. If they say, 'Take it,' I take."

He glanced at his watch, took a few quick puffs on his pipe, and then jumped up.

"I've been babbling the time away! The nine-o'clock train is almost here. Good night, good night."

And he quickly ran out.

Soon the windowpanes began to rattle, and the entire house groaned. They heard a few blasts from a whistle and saw thousands of sparks through the window. A train with small, dimly lit windows stopped for a while, then it began slowly chugging away. When the train was no longer in sight, they heard the whistle blasts again, as if the train were bidding farewell to the silent darkness.

"Do you think that the signalman got there in time?" Emil asked, concerned.

Once more, Karl shivered all over. He felt cold in every part of his body. He began to tremble. He sneezed once or twice, and then he was seized by a fit of sneezing.

"Are you cold?" asked Matilda.

"No, not all the time. Sometimes I feel cold and sometimes I feel warm."

All at once Karl remembered how once he'd left home in the pouring rain without his jacket. It seemed that he could hear his mother calling after him, "Karl, you'll catch cold! Karl! You naughty boy!"

He began to feel dizzy, and he grabbed onto a chair so that he wouldn't fall down.

Matilda felt his forehead.

"The boy is sick," she cried out, alarmed. "He's got a fever."

Hans stood up, blinking his eyes. He helped Matilda undress Karl.

Karl closed his eyes, and he said in a singsong, as if deep in sleep, "Aunt Matilda! I feel sick, Aunt Matilda! I love you. Emil! Emil! Hans! I feel sick."

Hans stood, his long arms at his sides, next to the bed where Karl now lay, his eyes shut.

chapter fifteen

Karl's eyes opened and shut perhaps a hundred times. He watched the dawn turn blue through the windows. He saw the day and then the dark of night. He even heard the train's whistle, but he responded to none of it, as if nothing mattered to him.

Karl didn't even know how many days had passed like this. He did remember that between opening and closing his eyes, Aunt Matilda stood by him with a spoon, which he had to take into his mouth. Only it wasn't always Aunt Matilda. Sometimes it was even his mother who nursed him, and other times it was the old Jewish man who sang his little tune as he gave him the bitter spoonful. Very often the old man sang just like a train whistle, and from time to time he stood on his head and shouted that his name was Hans.

But one thing Karl was sure of—someone was missing. He struggled to recall exactly who that someone was, but he just couldn't remember whom he had lost. He tried so hard to recall the face or at least the name of this missing person that drops of sweat broke out on his forehead.

It couldn't be that this someone's name was Karl. No, it certainly wasn't Karl! But just the other day he was crouching down on the ground next to this person, and they scrubbed the pavement with bleeding hands. But he couldn't recall how this person looked. At the very least, he wanted to remember his name, but he couldn't even do that.

Many times he had wanted to ask Aunt Matilda who it was that had dropped out of his memory, but each time that he was about to open his lips, his eyes fell shut.

Then one time Karl woke up in the middle of the night, and he smiled, because he remembered the word "Emil." He had no idea what this "Emil" was, but the word itself made him feel very happy, and he was glad that he remembered it.

A lamp was burning on the table, and Karl figured out that "Emil" was something else besides the lamp, something else besides the train whistle howling outside, just like someone who had puffed himself up with so much air that he turned red and then let out a wild scream.

Karl's eyes roamed around the room, looking for

something. He wanted to attach the word "Emil" to something, but it didn't belong to anything—not the table, not the lamp, not the window.

Suddenly he saw a bed across the room, and in that bed there was a face that looked just like "Emil." Just then, Karl felt that he was getting much better. He repeated the word "Emil" several times and looked at the bed, and even though he didn't completely understand what the word meant yet, he felt that he was about to figure it out.

Then suddenly he saw that near the bed, on a broken-down chair covered with a blanket, Hans was sleeping. His tousled red head lay there peacefully, his beard wasn't wild. He wasn't shouting or waving his hands about, and he wasn't laughing in that strange way he had.

In Hans's lap Karl saw an open book. Asleep, Hans looked so pleasant that Karl almost didn't recognize him.

Karl was sure he wasn't dreaming any longer but was seeing things as they were, because he had already seen Emil lying in the bed across from him—Emil, the very same person he had been missing all this time. But now it was Hans who was hard to recognize. There was something about him that was familiar, but then there was something that wasn't.

All at once Karl saw Hans stir and then wake up. He looked about the room, frightened. Karl shut his eyes halfway and noticed that Hans still looked very different. He saw Hans pick up the book and read it very attentively. Hans appeared to be deep in thought, and from time to time he ran his hand through his unkempt hair. Deep in thought, he took out a pencil and wrote something in the book.

When Hans got up from the chair and went over to the bed to take a look at Karl, the boy shut his eyes completely.

Hans walked about the room a few times, back and forth. He picked up another book and brought it over to the lamp. He stood and read; then once again he quickly took out a pencil and sat down at the table. He took a piece of paper from a drawer and began writing.

Karl started to get scared. He didn't understand what had happened to Hans, why he was so different. Karl made up his mind that the next day he would have to get out of bed. He stretched his legs and felt that he had the strength to do it. Under the covers he made a fist and was happy to see that it was strong, too.

He knew he'd been sick, but now he felt better. In the morning he would definitely get out of bed, and right away he would have to tell Emil the secret of how Hans behaved at night, how he became a completely different person, that he never shouted, not even once, but that he looked so nice and calm.

From the next room Aunt Matilda tiptoed in. Once more, Hans's whole body moved. Karl expected that Hans would shout *"Heil!"* or might even stand on his head.

"You should get some rest. Karl's feeling better," Matilda said.

But Karl wasn't paying attention to what Matilda was saying. He listened closely to find out how Hans would answer her.

And he was glad he listened, because Hans spoke, softly but clearly. Karl didn't recognize his voice at all.

"There's so much work, Matilda. So much to be done."

"Yes, but you must have the strength to work. You must have the strength to live."

"Don't worry, the devil won't get me," Hans answered, laughing.

He put out the lamp and started stretching his arms in all directions. It seemed as though he was doing exercises in the dark.

"It's already morning," Hans said.

"You can still get a few hours of sleep," Matilda replied, going back into the other room.

Hans dozed off in the chair. Karl lay there, petrified. He was afraid to move. He felt like crying. He didn't understand what had happened to Hans. He wished that it were already daytime, so that he could tell Emil about Hans's strange behavior.

chapter sixteen

In the morning Emil and Karl found a note from Aunt Matilda:

"Don't worry, boys, I'll be back in a few days. Hans will take good care of you."

Karl felt much better, though he was upset that Aunt Matilda had left the house. He thought about how many times she would get up in the middle of the night and cover him, and how many times she gave him a spoonful of medicine. Now he wanted to show her his thanks, but she was gone.

Karl's heart felt heavy. He fought against the feeling that perhaps Matilda might never come back again—like his mother, like all of the others who had been disappearing. He wanted to tell this to Emil but he held back, because Emil looked so worried. Karl knew that Emil missed Aunt Matilda terribly, too.

Karl also felt very grateful to Hans, who had stayed by his bed night after night, but the boy didn't know how to express his thanks. Now he found himself avoiding Hans. Karl couldn't look him straight in the eye—not after he'd seen Hans reading and heard how softly he had spoken to Matilda.

In fact, it seemed to Karl that Hans was avoiding him as well. He set the table, served breakfast, and let out one of his laughs now and then, even shouted *"Heil"* a few times, but Hans behaved differently from how he had in the park or on that first day when Karl and Emil came to the house.

Karl wanted to tell Emil everything that he'd seen the night before, but he waited. He didn't feel well enough to do that yet.

After lunch Karl sat in the warmth of the sun while Hans played ball with Emil. The ball flew back and forth, and Hans did some tricks. As the ball flew toward him, Hans did a somersault and still managed to catch it.

Karl wanted to join in their game, but Hans stopped him.

"Not healthy yet. Not healthy yet. Tomorrow!"

Hans stroked Karl's head and let out one of his sharp laughs.

Then Karl asked Hans if he would let him play ball for just fifteen minutes. Hans looked at him sternly and then broke out laughing.

"No. Aunt Matilda'll be mad."

"Where did Aunt Matilda go?" asked Emil.

"Back soon, back soon," Hans replied and did a somersault.

Emil had been playing for such a long time that he was drenched with sweat, and he decided it was time to stop.

All the while, Karl sat on the threshold, enjoying the sun. When Emil stopped playing, Karl asked Hans if he and Emil could take a short walk, just as far as the train tracks. The boys both promised that they would sit on the little hill near the tracks, and then, after watching a few trains pass by, they would come straight back.

"I'll shout 'Come back,'" Hans warned them, pointing his finger at Karl. "You're still weak."

Emil and Karl were lucky. As soon as they sat down on the little hill, a long train chugged by, and they counted the cars out loud.

"Thirty-two," the two boys shouted together, happy that they had both counted the same number.

Suddenly, Emil let out a sigh.

"What's the matter?" asked Karl.

"When I remember everything, I can't help it," Emil answered. "At night, when I think about my mother and father, I feel like crying. When you were sick I cried a lot, too."

"I was looking all around me then. I couldn't remember who you were or what your name was, but I knew that I missed you."

"We ought to find out what happened to our mothers."

"How can we do that?" Karl turned his large blue eyes toward Emil.

"I don't know, but we have to find out. We should ask Aunt Matilda. She knows everything."

"It might make Aunt Matilda very upset," Karl said. "She's been so good to us."

"But now she's gone," Emil said, trying not to sound upset.

"You know, Emil, I have something to tell you," Karl said. "I'll tell it to you, if you promise me that you won't get scared."

"Is it something very scary?" asked Emil.

"Very," said Karl. "I won't tell you now. I'll tell you when Aunt Matilda comes back."

"But I want to know what it is," Emil said. "Tell me a little bit at a time, not all at once."

Karl began to explain how he'd seen Hans reading books and even writing, and how Hans had spoken to Aunt Matilda in a soft voice, and that he had lots and lots of work to do.

"And you should have seen how he looked— completely different from before. His beard was different, his hair was combed, and his face looked so nice."

"And he didn't shout *Heil?*" Emil asked, amazed.

"Not once."

"That really is scary," said Emil. "I don't like it at all. Are you sure you weren't dreaming?"

"I'm a thousand times sure. After that, it took me a long time to fall asleep."

"And he didn't laugh and shout 'This is good?'" Emil wanted to know.

"No, not at all. He held his book up to the lamp, he read and wrote things down."

The signalman saw the boys. He waved to them from far away, but they didn't respond.

"I don't like him. Did you hear the story that he told us?" Emil asked.

"Look, he's wearing the yellow shoes he took from the shopkeeper," Karl said quietly.

Arm in arm, the boys started walking slowly back.

"You know what?" said Emil. "Tonight I'll stay up and watch what Hans does at night."

"You still don't believe me?" Karl asked, angrily.

"Oh, I believe you all right, but I want to see it with my own eyes."

"You'd be better off going to sleep," Karl suggested, "because you'll get scared."

"I'm scared at night anyway. I think about my mother. I can remember how she looked when they took her out of the house. You know what? Tonight, I'll plan to wake up in the middle of the night. But if I get really scared I'll wake you up."

"Yes," Karl agreed. "Tonight we'll sleep in the same bed. If you want to wake me up, just pull on my hair gently."

"OK!" said Emil.

"OK. Only don't pull too hard—just a gentle tug, and I'll open my eyes right away."

chapter seventeen

In the evening Friedrich, the signalman, came by. He sat down and blew clouds of smoke from his pipe. He was as drunk as he had been the last time. When he tried to speak, he could only utter fragments of words. He spoke to Emil and Karl, straining to make himself understood, but everything came out of his mouth so strangely that they kept laughing.

The signalman laughed with them. Between fits of laughter, he tried one more time to say something, but his tongue wouldn't do what he wanted.

And so he began to mumble to himself. It seemed as though he was asking himself a question that he himself didn't understand. When the boys burst out laughing, he couldn't help laughing, too.

Hans sat on the threshold. From time to time Emil and Karl looked at him, as if they expected something unusual to happen.

Then the signalman made a huge effort to say something. He struggled fiercely, until he was able to get a word out.

"Matilda?"

He punctuated the question with his pipe, using it to point at the room where Matilda usually slept.

"She'll be back soon," Karl answered.

The signalman was so happy that they understood him that he tried once more and asked, pointing to Karl.

"Better?"

"Yes, I'm all better now," said Karl.

The man took a penknife out of his pocket and offered it to him.

"Here, take it. A gift for you!" He opened it up and showed the boy that it had three blades and a corkscrew.

Karl looked at the shiny penknife and wanted to take it. But before he did he asked, "What about Emil?"

The signalman puffed on his pipe, pleased.

"Good boy! That's a good boy! Look—" and he took out another penknife, just as shiny as the first one.

"Two boys, two knives," he said, opening all the blades of the second knife as well.

Karl waited for Emil to take his penknife, but his friend didn't even move from his place.

"Here!" the signalman said to Emil. "It's yours."

"I don't want a knife. I don't need it," said Emil,

lowering his head. Karl stopped, surprised.

"Strange," said the signalman quickly, as if he had suddenly sobered up. "All boys like penknives, and these are nice ones, with corkscrews."

"I don't want a penknife," said Emil, his head still bowed. "You took those knives from someone."

The signalman jumped up.

"May God punish me if I'm not telling the truth. I bought these knives, one for Karl, and another for Emil. I haven't stolen any more things. That suit is still hanging in my closet, like a dead man. I've only put on these yellow shoes. The soles of my own shoes are completely worn out. I even put the watch away. It's just lying there like a sleeping monster, the hands stopped at ten after twelve. Look, this is still my old watch."

He took out his pocket watch and showed them. Suddenly he said, "Damn it, the ten o'clock train will be here soon."

And he ran out of the house, leaving both penknives on the chair where he had been sitting.

"He didn't steal the knives," said Karl, looking longingly at the open blades. "You heard, he swore that he didn't."

"I don't want them," Emil said, looking away from the chair. "He said that he stole some money, and he probably used that money to buy them. You can have your knife, if you want."

Karl went over to Emil. He wanted to say something, but he just stood there and looked at him, his eyes filled with tears.

"I don't need my penknife, either. My mother once bought me a penknife with four blades. It even had a little scoop for cleaning out your ears."

Emil didn't respond.

"You're my only friend," Karl continued, "and I'm the only friend you have."

"Yes," Emil answered. "Of course you're my only friend."

"Even though I really wanted to have my knife, I didn't take it," Karl said, apologetically.

"Yes, we're friends," Emil answered happily. "And we can play without knives."

Hans was still sitting on the threshold. He was leaning his head against the doorjamb. He breathed heavily.

Karl bent over and said softly, "He's sleeping. He's sound asleep."

Emil also bent over.

"He's asleep, all right. He must be very tired."

"He sat by my bed all night when I was sick. He must be worn out," Karl said, guiltily.

"I miss Matilda very much," said Emil, sighing. "She's so good; like Berta, maybe even better. Like my mother. When you were sick she cried, I saw it myself. Once she said to me, 'You know, Karl is very ill.'"

"I was really that sick?" Karl said, feeling important.

"Oh, you looked like you were dying. Do you know what I did?" Emil said softly, feeling embarrassed. "I said a prayer that my father taught me. I said it a few times before I went to sleep."

Karl sat down on the chair where the signalman had been sitting. Then he jumped up again, as if he had suddenly been bitten by something.

"I sat down on those stupid penknives. The blades almost cut me."

"We'll get rid of them tomorrow. He'll have to take them back," said Emil. "If not, we'll bury them in the ground."

"It's late. Let's go to sleep. Don't forget our plan," Karl said quietly, and he looked to see if Hans was still asleep.

"Of course I remember. I'll remind myself three times, and then I'll get up. I'm a little bit afraid, so don't get angry if I pull on your hair too hard. That'll be a signal that I'm scared."

"But not too hard, because I'll wake up and

scream and that'll ruin everything. Hans will find out that we're watching him."

They both got into the bed that Emil slept in while Karl had been sick.

"I wish there was someone to tell me a story now, or to sing me a nice little song. My mother knew a lot of lullabies," said Karl, and he began to hum a melody:

"Oy, yo, te, ti-di-di, daylom, daylom."

And Emil began singing along, "Ti-di-di, daylom, daylom."

"That's the Zeyde's tune," Emil said, happily. "Go on, sing it. I forgot all about it."

"Not me. I remember Zeyde's song really well," Karl said, humming the melody. "I'm never going to forget it."

chapter eighteen

In the morning when Emil opened his eyes, he felt embarrassed, because he had slept through the night.

"It's the first time that's ever happened to me," he told Karl. "Usually if I decide to get up in the middle of the night, I do it."

Karl laughed, but he reassured his friend.

"You probably tired yourself out playing ball."

Emil rested all day. When Hans invited him to play ball, he refused. But it didn't help; for a second night he slept soundly.

"I forgot how to do it," Emil complained. "This time I was sure I would do it. I shut my eyes tight, and I repeated to myself three times that I have to wake up in the middle of the night."

Karl thought it was funny that Emil's plan had failed twice.

"So why didn't you get up and wake me?" Emil protested to his friend.

Karl wanted to answer him, but just then the door opened and in walked Matilda.

Both boys shouted so loudly that Matilda was overcome.

They leaped out of bed and clung to her, making it impossible for her to move.

"Do you love me so much?" she asked, beaming with joy.

"Even more," answered Emil.

"We really missed you," Karl said.

Matilda was overwhelmed by their greeting. She looked taller than usual. Wisps of gray hair stuck out from under her hat. Her large, dark eyes sparkled with laughter, and she smiled broadly. Karl thought that Matilda was just as beautiful as his mother, even though she had a small scar under her left eye.

Just then Emil noticed that Hans was missing. He started to look around the house, but he was nowhere to be seen.

"Where's Hans?" Emil asked, concerned.

Karl ran from one room to the next and returned, surprised.

"Hans disappeared. Where did he go?" he asked, frightened.

"Don't be scared. He'll be back later, in the

evening," Matilda said, taking off her wet raincoat.

It was raining heavily outside. Matilda shut the windows to keep out the cold air. Suddenly it became dark, as if it were already dusk. She lit the lamp, and the room was filled with shadows.

"It isn't often that it's so dark during the day. It's only ten o'clock in the morning," Matilda said, as she gave each of the boys a glass of milk.

"And don't think that I forgot about you."

Matilda took out two penknives. She opened up both of them to show that they had four blades each. Not only that—each knife also had a little scissors.

Karl's eyes filled with tears. All at once he began to tell Matilda about the two penknives that Friedrich wanted to give them. Karl admitted that he was ready to accept the old man's gift, but Emil didn't want to. So they buried the knives near the house, with a piece of paper on which they had written, "Here lie two rotten knives."

"I'm so proud of you, boys. You cannot know how proud I am," Matilda said, drawing them close to her.

"And those penknives had only three blades," Emil said happily. "And they didn't have scissors, either."

Matilda gave the boys something to eat. When

they finished, and after they tried out their knives on pieces of paper, she explained that she wanted to tell them something—something extremely important.

"I've decided to tell you about a very serious matter," Matilda began. "I've thought a great deal about whether or not I should tell you, but your story about the penknives convinced me that I can, because you are such thoughtful boys.

"Vienna has become a completely different city," Matilda said.

"That's just what my mother told me," Karl said excitedly, as if he were hearing these words from his mother.

"Yes, your mother was right. This city is no longer recognizable. Don't think that there are only two children like you in Vienna. There are hundreds of Emils and Karls. In all of Austria there are many thousands."

Matilda sighed and then continued to speak.

"You're a little better off than the other Emils and Karls who don't even have a roof over their heads. They wander around, living from hand to mouth—hungry, naked, and barefoot.

"Our country is full of prisons now, tens of thousands of people have been locked up. They are suffering only because they dared to tell the truth.

Many people have been murdered. And the Emils and Karls are being persecuted, too. The Emils are suffering twice as much, because they are Jews. You saw how they were being treated that Sunday in the park."

"I was also treated like a Jew," Karl said proudly. "I had to wash the pavement with soap that burned my hands."

"Poor Karl, poor Emil, I don't know what to say to you. You already know everything. But I must tell you that this won't last forever. Thank God, we have Hans, and not just one Hans, but hundreds of Hanses."

"Hans?" Both boys cried out, shocked. "Do you mean our Hans?"

"Yes, our Hans," Matilda answered.

"I knew that something was going on," said Karl. "What did I tell you, Emil?"

"Hans was once a famous vaudeville actor. He entertained tens of thousands of people," Matilda explained. "But when Vienna began to change, he decided that the time for merrymaking had passed. He let his beard and his hair grow, so that no one would recognize him. It's all a disguise."

"You mean," Emil said, "that he's not—he's not—"

"No, he's not crazy. It's about time that you boys knew. You have no idea how it has tormented Hans that he has also had to deceive you. He'll be so happy when he returns tonight and finds out that he doesn't have to pretend in front of you any more."

Emil and Karl sat there, overwhelmed by what Matilda had told them.

All day long they asked her more questions. Matilda explained to them what Hans and his comrades were doing, how they risked their lives to distribute pamphlets and books, and how cleverly they went about this—how they printed pamphlets on cigarette paper, then wrapped them up and distributed them from house to house, how they made recordings of patriotic songs that ended with speeches denouncing the crimes of the current regime.

"And you, Aunt Matilda, what do you do?" Emil asked cautiously.

"I also help out. I do my share, too," Matilda said, shyly, like a little girl.

"But in order to organize the work against this brutal regime, we have to have underground meetings. As you can imagine, these meetings are very dangerous—deadly dangerous, but Hans and his comrades are strong and brave.

"In fact, tonight they're holding a meeting here in our house, in the room that we always keep dark," Matilda said. "Several dozen people will be coming. They'll get here late, just before midnight."

"I'd like to come, too," said Emil.

"Me too," Karl asked.

"If you're not tired, we'll let you come to the meeting."

Karl felt happy. It intrigued him that Matilda had called it an "underground" meeting. He remembered stories he'd once heard about underground caves and the sacks of gold and diamonds that lay hidden there.

"I wish it was already just before midnight," said Karl. "I can hardly wait."

Just then Hans appeared at the door. He stood there for a while and looked at Matilda.

"I've already told them all about it. It's better that way. Emil and Karl are our children. They've been through enough, and they ought to know about everything."

And as Matilda said these words, Hans went over to the boys and embraced them.

"My little friends, my little friends," Hans said, his voice trembling.

It was too much for Emil. He began to cry.

chapter nineteen

Just before midnight, Matilda put out all the lamps. Emil and Karl sat with bated breath and waited. Hans was already sitting in the windowless side room that was always dark.

The stillness upset Emil, and he moved close to where Karl was sitting. Matilda drew the drapes across all the windows. The only light in the house came from a firefly that had flown in by chance and flickered on and off.

Emil and Karl couldn't see Matilda, but they heard her breathing heavily. They could tell that she was waiting anxiously.

Karl found it very exciting to wait in the dark. He felt a tickling sensation in his throat. It had been quiet for such a long time that he wondered if anyone would come.

Suddenly the whole house began to shake. A train rushed by. They heard its whistle blow, then fade away. Long after the train, with its small, yellow windows, had passed by, they could still hear the whistle echoing from the little hill beside the tracks.

"That was the twelve-ten," said Hans from the dark room.

His voice came from out of the darkness unexpectedly. Emil and Karl trembled.

Aunt Matilda went over to the door and opened it. It grew a little lighter inside. Emil and Karl watched the door, full of anticipation. Matilda sat down between them, and all three kept their eyes fastened on the door, not saying a word.

Then the shadow of a man appeared and, without saying a word, he slipped into the dark room. A minute or two went by and another man came in, then another. One by one they came and vanished into the dark room. The last to arrive were two women. When Matilda saw them, she greeted them quietly and then closed the door.

"Perhaps you boys would like to go to sleep," Matilda said quietly.

"No," Karl replied. He felt as though his face was burning. He trembled all over with excitement.

"Not me," answered Emil, even more quietly and firmly.

Now Matilda, too, entered the dark room, and the boys approached as well. From inside the room they could hear Hans's powerful voice. He spoke quietly, but distinctly.

He explained that great discontent now reigned in Vienna. Mistrust was growing among the people. Many who had once looked forward to the new government with great hopes were now very disappointed. Hans revealed that their underground movement already had allies among the highest officials.

"How long will this last?" someone asked in a sad, dry voice.

Everyone remained silent. For a long time Hans did not reply.

"It depends entirely on us," said Matilda. "We must work harder and with more commitment. The day will come when we will dance for joy in the streets of Vienna and Berlin. Many of us will not live to see it. We will fall in battle, but it will have been worthwhile. This is an enormous struggle."

Emil and Karl drank in every word. To Emil it seemed as if the darkness had begun to glow all by itself. His eyes gleamed, like a cat that could see into every dark corner with glowing eyes. His heart pounded so loudly that he was afraid the others could hear it.

Karl was also caught up in the excitement of each word. It all seemed like an adventure story to him:

the darkness, the people, their speeches. He was so proud of Hans. It reminded him of the night he had seen Hans reading a book. He was also very glad that everyone listened so carefully to Matilda. She spoke calmly and so clearly that he understood each word. He couldn't see her face, but he knew exactly where she was sitting and followed the flow of her warm voice.

Next someone gave a report about a concentration camp. He described how people were tortured to death there. He had a list of the names of their comrades who had died there, people he had helped to bury. Many of them had dropped like flies from drinking the water, which was polluted. In the middle of the yard at the concentration camp there was also a pump with clean water, but it was for the guards only.

He told them more and more in a steady voice, until he broke down.

"Forgive me, friends," he sighed. "I'll be myself again soon. It's all still so fresh in my memory."

Karl thought about his mother. He was sure she was in a camp like that and was being tortured, just as the man had described.

"Soon you'll be free, Mama," he said quietly. "Hans and Matilda will take you away from there."

The commandant of the concentration camp offered one consolation to all the prisoners, the man continued to explain.

If you became tired and wanted to make an end to it all, there was a live wire in the prison courtyard. You touched the wire, and you died very easily.

That was what the commandant used to say to every new group of prisoners as they arrived at the camp by the hundreds. And many of them did choose this easy way out. But others decided that they had to live—to live.

The man finished his report, and everyone repeated the words: "Live! Live! Live!"

Emil and Karl could hear Matilda repeat the words in her gentle voice and Hans in his deep chest voice.

It was long past the end of the underground meeting. Emil and Karl lay in their bed and stared wide-eyed into the darkness.

They were silent. Emil wanted to ask Karl something, but he didn't dare. They heard the hoarse whistling of a train far away. In the darkness the boys felt Matilda pull the covers over them.

"Are you asleep, boys?"

Emil and Karl didn't answer. They didn't want to

say anything that would disrupt the silence.

"Matilda," said Hans, "perhaps it's too much for them to hear such things. They stayed up so late."

"There's no harm in it," Matilda answered. "They'll remember it when they're older. It will stay with them."

Emil was silent. It was too bad, he thought, that he wasn't older already.

Once more a train passed by. This time it made such a din that it seemed it might drag everything in the room along after it—the beds, the table, the bookshelves too.

Karl heard how the wheels of the train pounded out those three words, with which the meeting had ended:

Tra-ta-ta—Live!

Tra-ta-ta—Live!

Tra-ta-ta—Live!

chapter twenty

Karl woke up laughing. He'd had a happy dream and started to laugh while he was still asleep. He dreamed that his mother was tickling the soles of his feet the way she often used to when she woke him up to go to school.

His laughter also awakened Emil, who rubbed his eyes, wondering what was happening.

From the other room they heard Hans's voice. He was singing softly, as if trying not to wake them up.

Karl began to imitate Hans's deep voice. He sang so loudly that Hans, with his mop of hair and unkempt beard, appeared in the doorway.

"Lazybones!" Hans shouted. "Time to get out of bed and eat breakfast. Did my singing wake you up?" he asked, concerned.

"No," Karl answered, still singing. "Good morn-ing, Uncle Hans! Good morning, Aunt Matilda!" Karl sang out.

"Aunt Matilda's not here. She won't be back until

late tonight, so you have to eat whatever I give you."

"Aunt Matilda's no good," said Emil, still lying in bed. "She's always going away."

"Aunt Matilda has important work to do, very important work," Hans said, emphatically.

Emil suddenly remembered the meeting of the night before, and he no longer felt upset about Matilda. He was glad she was out at work. He was sure that whatever she was doing was necessary.

Emil and Karl dressed and ate quickly. The sun beckoned to them through the open door. They wanted to go outside and play ball as soon as possible.

"Today I'm a free man and can play with you," said Hans. "We can play for at least an hour, and afterward we'll take a walk in the woods nearby. I'll make each of you a walking stick, and then we'll hike and hike until we build up an appetite."

"Great!" Emil danced for joy. "It's been such a long time since we went for a walk. We'll have a good time today."

"You lazybones!" Hans shouted, pretending to be angry. "Don't you miss going to school?"

"I forgot all about school," Karl admitted.

"I haven't thought about it, either," said Emil.

"But that's just why Aunt Matilda and I have *not*

forgotten about it. We've decided that tomorrow you're going to get back to your studies. We'll make a real school, right here. We'll do it on a daily basis—one day I'll be your teacher, and the next day Matilda will teach you. Aunt Matilda knows a lot of nice songs, and I'll be in charge of giving out punishments. But for now, we'll forget about school."

Hans took them by the hand and led them outside. He took a ball from his pocket, and soon it was flying back and forth among them.

All at once, Hans froze. Emil threw the ball to him, but Hans didn't catch it. The ball rolled away, but Hans still stood there, immobile.

"I hear footsteps," he said, frightened. Karl also heard them, but he didn't understand why Hans had become so alarmed.

"That must be Aunt Matilda," said Emil.

"No," Hans replied, very quietly. "Matilda won't be back until very late."

The steps came closer, and within a minute Hans's face had completely changed. Now he looked just the way the boys had seen him that first time in the park, when the green and red leaflets went flying through the air. He broke out laughing in that peculiar way of his that Emil and Karl had forgotten.

"*Heil!*" he screamed with all of his might. "*Heil!*"

Emil and Karl couldn't take their eyes off him. They stood there, frozen. Suddenly they heard a heavy voice answer Hans with a "*Heil*."

A tall, middle-aged man stood near Hans. Hans did a somersault, then another one.

"This is good! This is good!" he shouted, and once more let out a laugh ending with a shriek that almost sounded like crying.

Suddenly, three more men appeared. One was fat, with a huge stomach. He went right up to Hans. Hans continued to shout "*Heil*" to each of the men. The fat man stood and looked at Hans, then shook his head and smiled.

"A very pretty comedy!" The fat man said to the other three, clapping his hands. "Excellent! Very amusing! But the game is over. Yes, the curtain has fallen. Bravo, bravo!" He clapped his hands, as though he were applauding a real play. "Viktor Schackeldorf, you can stop playing your comedy."

Hans stood up straight. He looked at all four men, as if he noticed them for the first time.

All at once he started to move.

"Stay right where you are," the fat man shouted with all his might, "or I'll shoot."

But it was too late. Hans punched one of the other men in the face. "Dirty traitor!" Hans said so quietly that he could barely be heard.

The man he struck moved slowly—almost as if he was expecting to be hit—and took out a hand-kerchief to wipe away the blood over his left eye.

"I couldn't help it, Schackeldorf," he said in a voice even lower than Hans's. "It's not my fault."

"I'm ready," Hans said. "Let me go into the house for just a moment."

"Absolutely not," said the fat man, drily.

"Not even if you go in with me?" asked Hans.

"No."

"Let me at least say good-bye to the children."

"No!" the fat man replied mechanically.

"In that case, then, I'm ready. Good-bye, Emil and Karl. Good-bye!"

The fat man ordered two of the others to go inside and inspect the house. They came out with some books and papers and lots of leaflets. The fat man took them and looked over each item separately. All the while he kept looking up at Hans, who stared back with sharp, piercing eyes.

A few minutes later, the five men seemed like five shadows. A train approached. When it left, they were no longer to be seen.

From the distance the signalman waved his little flag. He came straight over to the two boys.

"Who were those men that took Hans away?" he asked. Emil and Karl didn't respond.

"Where is Matilda?"

The boys said nothing.

"Did they arrest him? It's not true, is it?" he shouted, as if trying to awaken them from sleep.

Emil and Karl began to sob.

The signalman sat down on a rock. He smoked his pipe quietly.

"I'm an old man, I won't live much longer," he said, as though trying to comfort himself.

He inhaled and then let out a large cloud of smoke. "Did they really arrest Hans? Unbelievable!" he continued to argue with himself. "Funny! Ha!" He let out a sharp laugh. He puffed on his pipe and made a gesture with his hand.

"I'm an old man. It can't last much longer."

chapter twenty-one

Emil and Karl stopped crying. The old man sat there a while longer, but soon he got up and started to go.

"Today is Monday," he said. "In about five minutes a special freight train is going to pass through, then I'll be free for a few hours. I'll come back soon."

As soon as he left, Emil said, "We have to get away from here fast. There's no longer any reason for us to stay here. Hans is gone and Matilda's away. We've got to escape."

"But where should we go?" Karl asked, not moving from his place. "Friedrich just said that today is Monday," Karl thought to himself. It was the first time in a long, long while that he'd heard anyone say what day it was. Until now, many, many nameless days and nights had passed. But now it was Monday, the start of a new week. Everything was starting from the very beginning.

Emil and Karl went into the house. The main

room was no longer recognizable. Everything had been turned upside down. Apparently the two men had searched every corner to find those books and papers. They had even pulled up some of the floorboards.

"Where should we go?" Karl asked, as though in a dream. His eyes were still brimming with tears, and so it seemed to him that everything in the house was quivering—the chairs, the table, the window.

"Where?" he asked. "We could just stay here—today, and tomorrow, too, and the day after—and not eat anything. We'd just stay in one place and starve ourselves. Today is Monday, tomorrow is Tuesday, the next day is Wednesday—by then we'd probably die from hunger. We could die together—at the same time, at the same minute."

"No!" Emil shouted. "I don't want to die! I'm afraid to. Don't you remember, at the secret meeting, how they all shouted, 'Live! Live! Live!' When you're dead, you can't hear anymore or see anymore, but I want to see and hear everything."

"But everybody's dead," said Karl, as if he were sleeping. "My parents, your parents; Hans is probably dead now, too, and Matilda isn't here."

"Let's run away. Let's get on an express train," said Emil. "I'm afraid of the signalman. I'm afraid he'll try to poison us.

"Let's get away from here fast," he continued. "There must be a lot of others like us. Don't you remember? Aunt Matilda said that there were hundreds of kids like us, wandering around without any parents or friends. Let's find them, and then we'll all run away together."

Karl started to like the idea of looking for all those other children and then running off together. "Yes," he said, "We could all escape into the woods and live on fruits and nuts, and we'd get strong and hairy, like cavemen. And after we grow up we'll come back to the city, and we'll scare everyone, and we'll shout: 'Who killed our parents? Who killed Hans? Who arrested our friends?'"

Karl's eyes flashed, and he shouted louder. "'Who beat up the Jews?' We'll march together and shout, 'Who did it? Who?'"

Just then the signalman walked in. Emil and Karl started, as though someone had awakened them from a dream.

"Boys, I didn't mean to scare you. I'll take care of you, until I can turn you over to a good orphanage," the signalman said to Emil and Karl.

"No, we don't want any orphanage. We're scared of you, too. We're afraid you're going to poison us," Emil stammered.

"It's a sin to talk like that, Emil, it's a sin," the

signalman replied, with a broken voice. "I'm an old man, and I haven't done anyone any harm, except for the suit and the shoes that I took when I was dead drunk. I've lived my whole life all alone, with nothing but dry bread, a little milk, and a lot of whiskey—that's all. Now I'm old and sick, like a weather-beaten tree. My arms and legs ache. I don't remember my father, I don't remember my mother, I don't remember anyone, I have no one. So why should I do you any harm? Why? Two poor boys, all alone, just like me. Tell me, Emil, would I want to poison you?!"

Emil lowered his head. What the old man said had moved him. The signalman wiped the tears from his eyes with a dirty red handkerchief.

"Just look at what they did to this house. In one minute they turned everything upside down and inside out. They have no fear of God," the old man said. "We ought to clean up a little bit, before Matilda gets here."

He started picking up some of the overturned chairs.

"What do you think, Karl?" Emil asked softly. "Maybe we shouldn't run away just yet."

"Today is Monday," Karl thought. "There's no rush. Let's stay here until Tuesday or Wednesday."

"And what about food?" Emil asked, embarrassed.

"Well, in the meantime we can eat other things, until we can get to the nuts and fruit."

"Are you hungry?" the signalman asked. "I'll go and bring you some bread and a little milk, and a piece of cheese. I have some apples, too."

He left the house, and Emil and Karl watched as he ran breathlessly to his little hut by the train tracks.

"He's not a bad man," Karl said. "He's all alone, just like us."

"Yes," Emil agreed. "We could get used to him. We could stay with him for a few days. But we won't give up our plan to run off to the woods."

"Of course, that's our special plan," Karl said eagerly. "I can't wait until we escape to the woods."

A few minutes later Emil and Karl were sitting at the table. The signalman had returned and poured them foaming glasses of milk.

"I have a lot of time now, a whole hour and a half. Soon it will be dark. I have time until the express train comes. You know that train, the one that makes the windows in our houses rattle? My, but that is a fast train. It runs by like a wild man."

"We're going to run away soon, just like that!"

Karl suddenly shouted. "Hundreds of us, all covered with hair."

"Run away? Where?" The old man asked, terrified.

"Should I tell him?" Karl asked Emil, unsure of
himself.

"Of course, you can. There's nothing to be
scared of."

Karl beamed with excitement as he started to explain about the hundreds—which he now made out
to be thousands—that would come together and
shout, "Who killed our parents, who beat up the
Jews, who killed Hans? Who?"

"That's an very fine plan," the old man said
enthusiastically. "But by then I won't be in this
world any longer. Someone else will be living in my
little hut. It will still stand in the same place, the
trains will still go on running, and you'll shout,
'March! March! March!' But by then I'll be gone."

"You can't know that for sure," Emil comforted
him. "We'll grow up fast. We're going to live on
nuts and fruits. I had an uncle who only ate fruits
and nuts and vegetables, and he was as strong as
iron."

This pleased the old man, and his spirits picked
up. He began to march around the room, stamping
his feet. Emil and Karl followed after him, stamping

their feet in time with him. Karl yelled and all three of them turned toward the door, stretched out their hands, and shouted, "Who? Who? Who?"

The door slowly opened. With cautious, deliberate steps, Aunt Matilda entered.

chapter twenty-two

Emil and Karl were so surprised when they saw Matilda that they froze in place with their hands pointing at the door. They felt a little silly, but Friedrich, the signalman, was even more embarrassed. "We were just playing a little game," he explained right away to Matilda, who still stood at the door.

"Why are you standing there like that, Emil—and you, Karl? Aren't you at all glad to see your Aunt Matilda?" she asked in a hoarse voice.

The boys leaped over to her like two puppies, overcome with happiness. Only then did they notice that Aunt Matilda was dressed in old, torn clothes. She looked small and bent over, the way she did on that Sunday when they first saw her in the park, when they first saw Hans as well. Right away Emil realized that although she was trying to put on a happy face, Matilda's eyes were red and her face was pale, as if she had been crying all day.

Matilda looked around the room. She saw the

floorboards that had been pulled up. But before she stepped inside, she cast a sharp glance at the old man. Her eyes pierced through him, as if she was looking for an answer to a question that had been tormenting her—a question that she didn't even want to bring to her lips.

Emil and Karl noticed that Matilda looked suspiciously at the old man, who stood there helplessly, still pointing at the door—just as he had been while they were pretending to escape to the woods.

The signalman sensed that he was no longer welcome, and he began to move toward the door. He mumbled something and looked at Matilda, who still stared at him with penetrating eyes.

"No!" Matilda cried out in her hoarse voice. Her eyes flashed, like those of an animal at night. She stood up straight and thrust out her hand. "You won't leave here alive until you answer my question: Who turned Hans over to those bloodhounds?"

"Who?" she shouted, in the very same way that Emil and Karl and Friedrich himself had done earlier.

The old man hesitated. He gazed fearfully at a shiny pistol that Matilda aimed at him. He looked away from her, because he was much more afraid of her blazing eyes.

The old man seemed to sober up and he stepped

backwards, falling into a chair. But as soon as he collapsed into the little chair he became so small that he could barely be seen. Then a groan erupted from his crumpled body, and the expression on Matilda's face changed immediately. All her anger fell away, like a mask. She gripped the gun firmly in her hand.

"Why don't you shoot me, Matilda?" the old man wept.

"Make an end of it, finish me off. My life has already been eaten up, anyway," the old man said, sobbing.

But Matilda said nothing. She was satisfied to see that the old man wept. The more he cried, the more her face relaxed—not out of pleasure, but from a sense that she could trust him.

"Emil was afraid that I would poison him. You're suspicious of me, too. It's high time for me to die, it's long overdue."

Matilda believed him now, but still she said nothing. She wanted him to go on crying and talking, so that she could be sure of him.

Emil realized what was happening. Quickly, stumbling over his words as he often did, he explained everything to Matilda—how Hans was arrested, and how he'd punched someone in the face.

"What did the man look like?" Matilda wanted to know.

"He had gray hair, with a bald spot in the middle of his head," Karl said. "Hans called him a dirty traitor, and the man said that he didn't have any choice, he couldn't help it. Then Hans punched him hard."

"So *that* dog did it!" Matilda shouted. Her eyes blazed even brighter.

"Today, tomorrow, I'm going to throw myself under the wheels of an express train. No one needs me any more, no one believes me any more," said the old man, still sobbing.

"No, you won't throw yourself under a train. You have no idea how much you mean to me now, because you're not what I suspected you were. I had no idea who betrayed Hans. It's a terrible world, no one trusts anyone else. People are shooting each other in the back. When I came here I sneaked along the walls like a stray cat. I know that they're looking for me now, too. We've lost everything. We have to start all over again."

The signalman still sat there, hunched over. He didn't look up at Matilda, but he stopped crying.

"Where is Hans?" Emil asked.

Matilda didn't answer. She said nothing for a

long time. Finally, the old man got up and also asked, "Hans—where is he?"

"We've lost him," Matilda said, "We've lost him completely. They'll torture him to death. He didn't have a chance to take his own life before he fell into their evil hands.

"Did they arrest him in the house?" Matilda wanted to know.

"No, he wanted to go inside, but they didn't let him," Emil answered.

Matilda ran quickly over to the bookcase. She climbed up on a chair and pushed aside several books. Then she pushed against the wall, and one of the boards fell out. She reached her hand deep into the open space in the wall and took out a small revolver.

"You didn't wait in vain, my friend," Matilda said to the gun, as if it were a living thing. "You waited patiently for just such an opportunity, and it wasn't in vain."

Matilda got down from the chair and stood up straight.

"We mustn't waste any time now. I'm sure they're looking for me. I have to go away and hide for a few weeks, and I might have to leave Vienna altogether. Emil, Karl, it hurts me to say this to you, but we have to run away from here now, while it's dark. We'll leave by a different route."

She quickly took a blanket and wrapped it around Karl so cleverly that it covered him like a coat. Then she helped Emil into his coat.

The signalman stood there, stunned. He blinked his eyes.

"You're really leaving behind your house, Matilda? You're never coming back?"

"No, never. Good-bye, and please forgive me. It's not my fault. It's these times that are at fault; people have gone out of their minds."

Matilda gave him her hand.

"If they ask you, you don't know anything. You saw nothing, heard nothing."

"This house will stay empty," the signalman said to himself. Suddenly he noticed Emil and Karl.

"Good-bye, boys. When you run off to the woods, don't forget about our game. When you've grown up to be strong men, come by my little hut and knock on the door three times. If I'm still there, I'll come out and I'll go with you."

Matilda quickly looked around the house. Once more she ran over to the open space in the wall and took out a few books and some papers. She went over to the table and put out the lamp.

She stood in the darkness for a few minutes, as though it was somehow wrong for her to abandon the house. Emil and Karl and the signalman also stood there.

All at once the old man turned to go.

"I hear the ten o'clock train coming. I have to leave now. Good-bye."

Matilda took Emil and Karl, and together they set out on the road leading to the woods. The boys turned, and they could still see the open door of the dark house. Matilda stopped for a moment and she, too, looked back at the door, which seemed to be calling them back reproachfully.

All at once there was a strong gust of wind. The door slammed shut, and the house stood there, a part of the silent darkness all around.

chapter twenty-three

"I wonder what time it is," Matilda said.

The boys held onto her firmly. They wanted to start running fast, but Matilda held them back.

"Don't be afraid, these woods are small and not very dense. It looks a lot thicker at night than it does during the day. During the day you can even see right through the trees to the houses on the other side."

"It must be after ten by now," said Emil. "The signalman ran to meet the ten o'clock train."

"Yes," said Matilda, stroking his head in the dark. "I forgot all about that. Still, I should have taken the clock with us. A clock can come in handy."

Karl felt in his pocket and was glad to discover that he hadn't forgotten the penknife that Matilda had given him.

"Do you have your knife?" he asked Emil.

"Of course I have it. I never take it out of my pocket. I'm afraid I might lose it."

"Are there any animals in the woods?" Karl wanted to know.

"Maybe some stray cats," Matilda said, laughing. "In the daylight you could see that there's not much to these woods. But at night it looks like a real forest. There used to be some big, thick trees here, but they were cut down long ago."

"And the Erlking*?" asked Emil. "Can the Erlking come into the forest?"

"The Erlking is just a foolish bit of make-believe. Somebody made it up just to scare children. You don't have to be afraid of anything. We'll be on the other side soon.

"But when we reach the other side," Matilda continued, "You must walk slowly, as if you're out taking a stroll. You mustn't run. If you start running, then they'll start to chase after us."

"What if we see a wolf with fiery eyes?" Karl said, more to himself than to Matilda.

"A wolf wouldn't come so close to the city. The trains passing by would frighten it so much that it would run away. Anyway, if some animal does come near us, I'll fire at it. I have two guns with me, and they're both loaded."

*The Erlking is a mischievous spirit in German folklore who is said to harm little children.

Karl was silent. Emil said nothing, either. He remembered how Matilda pointed the revolver at the signalman, and he felt a pang in his heart for the old man.

"It's too bad!" he said out loud. "We should have taken the signalman along with us. He's so lonely."

Karl sighed. Suddenly something moved and landed at Karl's feet. It flapped its wings, and then they heard it fly away.

Emil and Karl stood still, petrified with fear.

"Silly boys, you're just as scared as that owl was. It was sleeping in that tree."

"Where are we going?" Emil asked, still somewhat afraid.

"Look, here we are, out of the woods already," Matilda said happily.

After walking the entire way with their heads lowered and eyes half shut, Emil and Karl looked around.

In the distance they saw several little fires burning. It was hard for them to get used to seeing in such low light after walking blindly through the woods. Now they could clearly see a few small houses below them in a valley. Emil and Karl started to race happily down the hill.

"Didn't we agree not to run?" Matilda scolded them.

Emil and Karl slowed down. The sky grew a little brighter. Here and there tiny stars twinkled and then disappeared, like bright spangles.

"We're heading back into the city now, but by another route," Matilda said. "In about fifteen minutes we'll reach the place where you'll spend the night."

"Will you stay there with us?" Karl asked.

"No, tonight it won't be safe for me there," Matilda said. "I'll have to go somewhere else, but you'll have a nice place to sleep."

Emil didn't even want to ask what sort of place it was. He no longer cared. It was all the same to him wherever he was being taken. Even if it was a dark cellar, he thought, like the one where he and Karl wound up spending the night. He remembered the kitten that curled up with him then.

If only he could be a kitten that didn't need a home, didn't need a mother and father. But soon he would no longer need a home, either. He'd already become used to the idea that when he'd find a new home, something would happen and he'd have to move on once more.

Tomorrow morning he'd try to learn where his mother was. He had to know what had happened to her. He knew what had become of his father. He'd been at the funeral, with his mother and uncle. But his mother had been taken away, and that was all he knew.

"It must be very late by now," Emil said, sighing.

A clock responded to his question with eleven strokes, sounding as though someone was pounding with a hammer eleven times.

"Silly, did you hear that? It's just eleven o'clock. We've been on the road for less than an hour," Matilda said. "At night everything seems bigger and longer.

"We have three more blocks to go," she continued. "We're going to my sister-in-law's house. Her husband was my brother. Thank God, he died a year ago and didn't live to see all of this turmoil. My sister-in-law is Jewish," she said, bending over to Emil. "She works at an emigration center. She helps people escape from here. After the present government persecutes them and takes away everything they have, it kicks them out of the country. The lucky ones can find a new country that will open its gates to them.

"Each week," Matilda said very quietly, "They send off several hundred boys and girls just like you, who have no parents, no friends. Tomorrow they're sending away another very large group. Emil, Karl, you're among the lucky ones. It's easier to save children. There are many sympathetic countries: England, France, Holland, Belgium, America. You have to escape, while there's still time."

This made Karl feel happy. His heart was warmed by the list of countries that Matilda had named. England, France, Holland, Belgium, America—they were like stars, little spangles that glistened for a moment and then disappeared into the darkness.

"And will you be going with us?" Karl asked.

"No, I can't. And—" Matilda paused for a while—"I mustn't. I have to stay here. I have to stay here, along with hundreds, thousands of others. Now we live like mice, hiding in holes, but one day, somewhere, you'll hear the good news that Vienna is Vienna again, and Berlin is Berlin again, and people are living like human beings once more. Meanwhile, we have to save you. If you stay here, you won't survive."

Emil listened closely, but he felt numb. It was a sensation that often came over him, ever since that day when his mother sat on the footstool and didn't move, didn't even speak.

Matilda stopped in front of a small house. She took out a key, walked up a few steps, and unlocked the door.

The face of a frightened young woman appeared at the entrance. She herded Matilda and the two boys inside.

Once inside, they all felt at home. The house was cozy and tidy. The woman's eyes, warm and dark, were brimming with tears. They looked as though they were about to burst. The young woman embraced Matilda and began sobbing quietly.

chapter twenty-four

The next morning it was raining heavily. Emil, Karl, and Matilda's sister-in-law walked under a large umbrella. The umbrella had a few holes in it, and raindrops kept landing on the back of Emil's neck. No matter where he moved, a drop managed to find him.

Karl began to shiver. He still had no coat to wear. Matilda's sister-in-law had wrapped a white scarf around his throat, but he still felt cold. The woman said nothing, and neither did Emil or Karl.

Everything had happened so quickly since the night before. Emil was unable to tie it all together. He couldn't remember when he'd gone to sleep, or even when he'd undressed. Nor could he recall when he'd awoken. He felt as if he were still dreaming, and only the drops of rain falling on his neck every now and then kept him awake.

Quietly he asked Karl if he remembered when Matilda had left, but Karl could only remember that he'd heard her talking to her sister-in-law at night, when he was already in bed. He'd heard her talking about Hans's arrest. He'd even heard Matilda's sister-in-law say that they would execute Hans for sure. That was all Karl remembered. He'd been so tired that when the woman woke him he thought he hadn't been asleep for more than a minute.

Matilda's sister-in-law bent over, still holding the umbrella, and warned them that it would be better if they didn't talk, so as not to attract any attention.

Emil and Karl walked along unfamiliar streets. The houses were drenched with the rain, the horses were soaking wet, people looked angry and tense.

Cars raced by and splashed through streams of water. Policemen, their raincoats soaking wet, stood impatiently, directing traffic. Everywhere children who were late hurried off to school.

When Emil saw these children, he let out a deep sigh. Karl knew at once what his friend was feeling. Those children were happy. They tramped through puddles of dirty water with their galoshes.

Matilda's sister-in-law turned down a small alley. It seemed as though the little street had no space in the middle. The walls on either side almost touched each other. The woman walked up a short flight of iron steps. When she opened the door, Emil and Karl were amazed at what they saw.

There, in a large, dark hall, sat more children than they could count. They sat on long benches and held little bowls on their laps, eating silently. The boys sat separately from the girls.

Immediately Matilda's sister-in-law turned Emil and Karl over to one of the women who supervised the children. She squeezed the two of them onto a crowded bench and served them hot soup and pieces of bread.

"Do we have milk today?" Matilda's sister-in-law asked, in a dry voice.

"Maybe we'll get some later," the supervisor answered. "There isn't any just now." Matilda's sister-in-law took off her coat, put on a pair of glasses, and sat down at a small table.

The windows were covered with rags and old blankets. Only a few small lamps burned in the large hall. This gave it an inhospitable feeling and caused everyone in there to shiver, as if they were outside in the rain. The silence was broken occasionally by sobbing. The younger children cried loudly, and the women who distributed the soup could barely comfort them.

Four or five women opened the door quietly, but Matilda's sister-in-law jumped up right away and stopped them at the entrance.

"Ladies, please, you must leave, we can't make any exceptions. You know our situation."

The women asked if they could at least have one last look at their children.

"We can't, it's not permitted, we mustn't have any scenes. You can see your children at exactly twelve-thirty, at the train." And with that she forced them out of the room.

"I've told you a thousand times that we can't allow any mothers inside," she said sternly to the supervisors. "Our entire office could be shut down. You know the rules just as well as I do."

When the children finished eating, Matilda's sister-in-law told them all to remain sitting in their places. She stationed herself in the middle of the room and explained to the children that in a few hours they would be leaving Vienna for good. Calmly she explained that before the train would leave, those children who have parents would probably be able to see their mothers and fathers at the station. The children leaving today would be going to England.

Emil felt cold and then warm at the thought that he was leaving Vienna. He wished he were already at the train. He thought that perhaps his mother might somehow come to say good-bye to him at the station.

Karl wanted to say something, but he felt that Matilda's sister-in-law was looking at him from behind her glasses.

"You mustn't cry. Those who feel like crying can remain here. In an hour you'll go by bus to the train station. If you have any friends here, we advise you to write notes to each other. It often happens that good friends get sent to different cities, even different countries. So it wouldn't be a bad idea if you wrote each other a few words now."

Once more it seemed to Karl that the woman was looking at him and Emil. The supervisors gave out pencils and pieces of paper, and many of the children started writing notes.

"But there's no way that they'll separate us," said Emil.

"No way at all," Karl responded firmly. "I'll hold onto your sleeve, and I won't let go. We'll stick together."

"Should we write each other a letter?"

"I guess so," said Karl, and he picked up a pencil.

As soon as he held the pencil in his hand, Karl was overcome with happiness, and he started writing:

Dear Emil,
    We'll never let anyone separate us.
    We'll be friends forever.
        Your dear friend,
          Karl

He held the letter for a while and then turned to give it to Emil. But Emil was still bent over his piece of paper. Tears ran down from his eyes—such big tears that the brittle piece of paper was stained with spots.

"I can't write any more, I can't," he said to Karl, and he gave him the letter, in which he had written only the first few words:

> *To my only friend, Karl.*
> *I*

But the words were spotted with tears, and after the word "I" there were so many stains that the piece of paper was wet.

Now Karl didn't feel ready to hand over his letter. He wanted to cover it with tears, too, but his eyes felt dry and hard.

Matilda's sister-in-law raised an old blanket that hung over the window and called out, "We're leaving!"

chapter twenty-five

Emil and Karl jumped up from their places. Right away they grabbed each other by the hand, as if even then someone was about to separate them.

Five buses were waiting outside the building. The rain had stopped, but the sky was still dark gray and looked ready to start pouring again.

On both sides of the buses stood several dozen men and women, both young and old, who were shouting in unison.

"Jews, go to Palestine! Dirty Jews to Palestine!"

Some of the teenagers in the crowd began pelting the buses with stones. The youngest of the children started crying, but the women quietly helped them onto the buses.

A small stone hit Matilda's sister-in-law in the head. She started, but she didn't even turn around and she continued with her work.

Shouts of "Jews, go to Palestine!" could be heard even from the rooftops, where dozens of boys and girls were standing. The children getting on the buses looked up out of curiosity. Paper bags filled with water crashed down from the roofs. The bags burst open and hit a few of the children on the head.

Someone in the middle of the crowd turned on a hose and aimed the water at the children and the drivers. The crowd roared and went crazy. Some became so wild that they went right up to the children and pulled them by the hair, kicked them, and slapped them.

Suddenly Karl felt a shove. A woman, staggering like a drunkard, stood next to him. In the commotion she pressed something in his hand.

He looked closely at her, and he cried out, "Mat—"

But he stopped. He saw her put her hand over her mouth and look at him, smiling through tear-filled eyes.

He tugged on Emil's arm. Emil also looked around.

"Karl, that's—"

"Yes," Karl said, cutting him off, as though he were Emil's older brother.

Emil also caught a glimpse of Matilda's smile, but in an instant he watched her twist up her face to look like a drunkard, and she shouted, "Jews, go to Palestine!"

When the buses were loaded and on their way,

Emil said quietly to Karl, "She risked her life to come see us."

"Yes, she's so brave! She gave me a piece of paper. I have it here."

Karl opened his hand.

"Two pieces of paper!" he whispered. "On one it says 'Emil' and on the other is 'Karl.'"

Karl gave Emil one of the folded pieces of paper. Quickly he opened up his.

> *I will die so that Emil and Karl might be able to live together in peace.*
>
> *Hans*

Karl shivered with cold.

"What does your note say, Emil?" Karl asked impatiently.

Emil hastily opened his piece of paper with trembling hands.

> *I will die so that Emil and Karl might be able to live together in peace.*
>
> *Hans*

Emil and Karl looked at each other in silence and, without saying a word, buried the notes deep in their pockets.

Karl began to wonder how Hans had sent these notes to them, and how they came just as he and Emil were about to go away. Emil also seemed to be thinking about the same thing, because he quietly answered Karl.

"Matilda's very brave."

"Oh," said Karl with a burst of happiness, "she's braver than brave."

The buses bounced hurriedly over cobblestone streets. It felt as if they were still being pelted with stones and were trying to run away from the city as fast as they could.

It seemed to Karl that the buses' rushing over the pavement sounded like "Vienna! Vienna! Vienna!"

He thought about his mother. She must already be dead. She, too, died so that Emil and he might live together in peace.

Mama!

Karl was sure that she would have written a note like that to him and to Emil before she died.

He thought about his father's picture that had hung in their house. Who knew where that picture was now?

"Vienna! Vienna! Vienna!" the buses growled. His mother had lived in Vienna, his father had lived in Vienna, but soon he would no longer live there. He had to escape.

There was such a din at the train station that Emil trembled. It reminded him of the terrible commotion when he and Karl had scrubbed the pavement.

Storm troopers and policemen were herding everyone into the waiting room. Women and men embraced their children, weeping. Some women fainted and were left lying in the middle of all the chaos. Storm troopers kept pushing the children toward an open door, through which they could see a train with many cars.

Karl still held on to Emil with a firm grip. The storm troopers were now letting through adults, who had papers to show them. The soldiers examined their papers carefully, inspected their luggage, then gave them a shove or a kick and let them through to the train.

Emil and Karl now stood near the door. All at once Emil tugged on Karl's sleeve. Karl looked around and saw that the last of the adult passengers to go through was the old man who had scrubbed the pavement with them. All at once the melody that the old man had sung to them then began ringing inside Karl's head.

"Oy, yo-te-ti-di-day, daylom, daylom."

He remembered the whole melody from beginning to end.

"Do you see? Zeyde's also going away!"

Karl began humming the tune, as though he wanted the old man to be able to hear it.

"Be quiet," Emil advised. "We can sing it later on the train."

Emil and Karl could hear the old man explain to a soldier that his grandson was bringing him to America.

"Oh, to the Jewish President Roosevelt!"

"What?" the old man repeated, blinking his eyes.

"What!?" The storm trooper became enraged and hit the old man so hard that he fell to the ground.

He picked himself up, smoothed himself out, and started running toward the train, but then he stopped and went back.

"Hit me again!" he said to the storm trooper.

"Hit you again? Why?" the soldier asked, turning red.

"I want to be sure to remember this. You hit me too quickly. Give me another one. A present like that is worth remembering."

The soldier raised his foot, but instead of kicking the old man he started shouting wildly. "Get on the train now, or else I'll shoot you like a dog."

The old man picked up his satchel and walked to the train.

All of a sudden there was a great deal of running

and jumping about. The soldiers opened the door and let the children through. Mothers and fathers raced toward the open door, weeping. The soldiers went berserk. They kicked and shoved the children, who fled, panic-stricken, into the train.

Then all at once the conductors closed the doors to the cars of the train and shouted to the soldiers, "There isn't room to breathe in there!"

"Push more of them in. So what if they choke."

"Impossible!" the conductors gestured.

Then the soldiers raised their right hands in salute.

"Move on out!"

Karl broke away from his place. Frightened and impatient, he felt his entire body trembling, as if he were about to explode.

He shouted at the top of his lungs, but no one heard him in the midst of all the commotion. He tried to shout louder than everyone else.

"Emil! Emil!"

Emil was no longer next to him. He'd been pushed away and shoved into the train.

The train began to pant, like a huge dog. Huff-huff-huff. Karl watched the train, hoping at least to catch one last glimpse of Emil.

The cars of the train rolled by. They were dark;

he couldn't see anyone. It seemed as if the train had devoured them all.

About forty children and a dozen adults remained standing on the platform. They wanted to go back into the waiting room, but the storm troopers had shut the doors.

"Another train will arrive in three hours."

Karl felt a sharp pang of hunger in his stomach. He gnashed his teeth.

It started to rain again. The adults moved the children under the narrow roof covering the platform. Karl fidgeted. He couldn't stay in one place. A voice inside him kept shouting, "Emil! Emil!"

Three more hours in Vienna.

A thirteen-year-old girl with straw-blond hair, a pug nose, and bright blue eyes was eating an apple. She took another apple out of a paper bag and offered it to Karl. He bit into it.

"I'm sure we'll get on the next train," she said, with a grown-up expression.

"My friend left on the first one," he said, and he ate the apple quickly, because he was afraid that otherwise he would start crying.

Karl put his hand in his pocket and discovered that he still had the two letters, the one from Emil and the one from Hans. This made him feel a little happier. It seemed as though he wasn't completely alone, because he had his two friends with him.

He thought about Emil's note, stained with teardrops. It was too bad—now it would be so easy for him to cover his letter to Emil with tears. It felt as though he would burst into tears any minute.

"We still have two hours until the train comes," the girl with the bright eyes told him.

"Two more hours in Vienna!" Karl thought.

He imagined that his father's picture had just fallen off the wall. The walls collapsed, the whole building crumbled. Emil's building also fell down; all the buildings in Vienna had toppled over. All the people were buried under the stones that were falling everywhere, raining down on them from all sides, even from the rooftops. The only ones left were those few children and adults who stood there, waiting for the train.

"Will I really get on the next train?" he asked the girl who had given him the apple.

"You can be sure of it," she replied. "Isn't that right?" she asked an old woman who stood nearby.

The woman sadly nodded her head.

Afterword: About *Emil and Karl*

There have been many novels about the Holocaust for young readers, but this one is different. The others were written following the end of World War II, sometimes decades after the events they describe had taken place. *Emil and Karl*, however, was written about the experiences of European Jews and their neighbors living under Nazi occupation while these events were still happening. In fact, it is among the very first books written about the Holocaust for readers of any age and in any language. Therefore, it offers a special perspective on this chapter of history. The story of the author of this novel and of the children for whom it was originally written also helps us understand what is distinctive about this book.

Yankev Glatshteyn, the author of *Emil and Karl*, was born in 1896 in the Polish city of Lublin. In addition to studying in a *kheyder*, the traditional religious school where Jewish children learn to read

Hebrew, Glatshteyn also received a modern educa-
tion from private tutors. At the age of eighteen he
immigrated to America, as did many thousands of
other East European Jews. Glatshteyn settled in New
York City, where he studied law. But instead of pur-
suing a career as a lawyer, he became a writer. In
1920, together with a circle of friends that he met
in New York, he formed a group of writers who
were dedicated to writing modern poetry and fiction
in their native language, Yiddish. The group called
themselves the *Inzikhistn*—the Introspectivists—
because they thought it was important for authors
to reflect their own inner, personal feelings and
experiences in whatever they wrote.

At that time Yiddish was the first language of
most of the millions of Jews living in the United
States, Canada, Mexico, Argentina, England, France,
Poland, Hungary, the Soviet Union, and other countries. Cities and towns on both sides of the Atlantic
had neighborhoods full of Jews who spoke Yiddish
with one another at work, on the street, and at
home. They read Yiddish books and newspapers, listened to Yiddish on the radio and sound recordings,
went to see Yiddish theater and movies, and joined
political and religious organizations that were run in
Yiddish. Many Jewish children went to schools and

summer camps where they learned to speak, read, and write in Yiddish. Glatshteyn and other Yiddish writers treasured the language as an important part of their Jewish cultural heritage. At the same time, they used Yiddish as a modern literary language—a language for discussing all sorts of contemporary issues and for expressing their own ideas.

In 1934, Glatshteyn learned that his mother, who still lived in Lublin, was very ill. He decided to return to Poland to visit her. During this trip he saw how much Jewish life in Europe had changed in the twenty years since he had left for America. On one hand, there was much to be excited about; Jews were involved in modern cultural, social, and political activities in ways that had never before been possible. On the other hand, there was also cause for grave concern. Discrimination against Jews was a growing problem in many Central and East European countries. Polish Jews were increasingly the victims of economic boycotts and physical attacks; often their complaints to authorities met with little sympathy. In the Soviet Union, Jews were finding that the government's early promise of support for Yiddish culture was now met with more and more opposition by the state. Most threatening was the rise of Adolf Hitler, head of the Nazi Party, to the position of Chancellor of Germany in 1933. Hitler's regime was outspoken in its anti-Semitism, and it enacted numerous laws that denied Jews their rights as German citizens. The Nazis regarded Jews as a race, rather than an ethnic, national, or religious group. Moreover, Nazis considered Jews an inferior race compared to Aryans—whom they felt were the true "native" population of Germany—and they blamed Jews for causing Germany's social and economic problems.

When Glatshteyn returned to America, he wrote about his trip and the observations he had made about Jewish life in Europe in two novels written for adults. At the same time he also wrote *Emil and Karl*, a book especially for younger readers. It was published in New York in February 1940. By then, the situation in Europe had worsened. Nazi Germany had invaded Poland on September 1, 1939, beginning the World War II.

Emil and Karl takes place in Vienna, the capital of Austria, some time shortly before the war began. In March 1938, Germany annexed Austria, claiming that it was doing so on behalf of the Aryans living there, in order to create a larger, more powerful nation for all "true" German people. Most of Austria's Jews lived in Vienna at that time. Like the

Jews of Germany, they too were persecuted by the Nazis. In fact, the Nazis enacted anti-Semitic policies much more swiftly in Austria than they had in Germany. Within a matter of weeks, Jewish organizations were abolished and their leaders were arrested, Jewish property was seized, and many Jews were forced to leave their homes. In addition, Jewish people were often publicly humiliated and physically attacked, both by Nazi officials and by Austrian citizens who sympathized with Nazi policies. Incidents described in *Emil and Karl*, such as Jewish shops being looted, Jews being forced to scrub Vienna's streets with their bare hands and to act like animals in a public park, actually happened and were reported in American newspapers.

Most Austrian Jews tried to flee the country, but they found it increasingly difficult to do so. Even if they were able to get out of Austria, they often found no other country that would welcome them. As a result, many of Austria's Jews were deported to concentration camps and, later on during the war, to death camps.

The Nazis also considered other groups of people besides Jews to be their enemies. Socialists, like Karl's father and mother in this novel—as well as communists, Jehovah's Witnesses, homosexuals, and Gypsies—were also persecuted. Some of those who were opposed to Nazism organized efforts to overthrow the Nazi control of the government and to encourage ordinary people to resist Nazi teachings and policies. Because Nazis tolerated no opposition to their ideas, this was a risky undertaking. Like Matilda and Hans in the novel, those who were against Nazism often organized in secret. Many of those who opposed Nazism or who simply were the kinds of people whom Nazis considered unfit members of society were arrested, tortured, and even executed.

Writing this novel at the beginning of World War II, Glatshteyn did not know the terrible fate that most of Europe's Jews would suffer during the war. At that time, many people were hopeful that the majority of Jews threatened by Nazi persecution would somehow be rescued. Thousands of men, women, and children were, in fact, able to find new homes in other countries around the world, although as the war progressed this became less and less possible. As in this novel, some children managed to escape Nazi-occupied countries thanks to the special efforts of government agencies and private citizens committed to their rescue. Many of the millions of European Jews unable to escape the Nazis dedicated their lives to fighting Nazism with all their might, and some were able to survive the enormous effort that was made to murder them. Despite all these hopes and acts of courage, millions of Europe's Jews lost their lives during this terrible period, as did many of the other people the Nazis had set out to destroy, before Germany was defeated in 1945.

Therefore, it is hard to say what might have happened to Emil and to Karl—if they had been real children—by the end of World War II. Nevertheless, their story is as important for us to read today as it was when Glatshteyn wrote it. *Emil and Karl* shows us how differently people responded to the hatred and intolerance that Nazism propagated. While many did nothing to resist it or even to question its principles, there were those who abhorred these atrocities. Some were too afraid to challenge Nazi authorities, but others fought against them, risking their lives.

Although German would be the language that Emil, Karl, and the other characters would have spoken to each other in Vienna, Glatshteyn wrote this book in Yiddish. Yiddish was not only Glatshteyn's native language; it was also at the center of a modern Jewish culture that he had devoted his life to enriching through his poems and novels. Glatshteyn dedicated *Emil and Karl* to his children,

Saul, Naomi, and Gabriel. The book was also intended for the thousands of other American Jewish children who knew Yiddish. Many of them read *Emil and Karl* while attending one of dozens of afternoon and weekend Yiddish schools that were located in major cities around the country. From this book they learned about the persecutions then being inflicted on Europe's Jews—a subject most other American children didn't study in school at the time. But Glatshteyn and other American Jews felt that their children needed to know what was happening to their fellow Jews, including youngsters their own age, across the Atlantic.

By writing a story about two boys—one who is Jewish, the other who is not—Glatshteyn also wanted his young readers to understand that what was happening to Jews in Europe had an impact on everyone living there, and that the future of Europe's Jews depended on their relationships with their non-Jewish neighbors. And so those first readers of *Emil and Karl* learned from this novel— as we do today—of the importance of friendship, of tolerance, and of bravery.

Jeffrey Shandler
New York